This book is due for return on or before ~~...~~ Libby Hathorn

h

Hodder
Children's
Books

a division of Hodder Headline plc

Copyright © 1994 Libby Hathorn
Cover illustration by Gregory Rogers

First published in Australia and New Zealand in 1994
by Hodder Headline Australia Pty Ltd

First published in Great Britain in 1996
by Hodder Children's Books

A Catalogue record for this book is available from the British Library

ISBN 0 340 65124 5

Typeset by Avon Dataset Ltd, Bidford-on-Avon, B50 4JH

Printed and bound in Great Britain by
Cox & Wyman Ltd, Reading, Berks

Hodder Children's Books
a division of Hodder Headline plc
338 Euston Road
London NW1 3BH

PROLOGUE

He longed to see the river because he hadn't ever seen one; because he instinctively knew of its strength and its possibilities. But most of all because of his grandmother.

He dreamt of it, a long sinuous bandage of glittering water tumbling down from some frothy mountain start, stretching outwards across the countryside. Going fast sometimes but mostly nice and easy.

A river would unravel across the land in its own time with boats and jetties making little difference. Minding its own business on its way to the sea.

The way his grandmother had told him *her* river flowed past the door when she'd been a little girl so far away in another country. Lots and lots about her river. Her river from start to finish.

His grandmother had rocked him, when he was a little boy, after attending to his bruised lip or his hurt eye. She'd soothe away the pain with her talk. 'Oh the river, sonny boy, where I grew up,' she'd say in a kind of singing voice and he'd let himself be rocked

'It's lovely at a river. But my river—my river's lovely beyond believing! And one day I'm going to take you away from here. Far away. I'm going to show you that old river. And everything will be wonderful, once we get there. That's for sure.'

Morning

He wakened to an unfamiliar sight.
A soaring ceiling of corrugated iron,
Held up by a web of metal beams.
Glass windows, set in the iron.
Through the glass he could see sky.
A grey space, interrupted
with odd fluttering movements
now and then.
Birds! Birds flying over the great domed ceiling.
Where was he then?
When he moved he remembered.
(He felt the hard plastic bench beneath him.)
Oh, he was stiff all over!
He moved his bruised shoulder cautiously,
his aching joints,
hurting as they had
in that wet, dark tomb
he wanted so much to forget.

The place he'd been buried in
for the past two days.
Yes, he was stiff and his body ached.
But his heart was light, light!
He wasn't in that blackness any more.
He was in a place with a domed roof
with birds flying over,
a place that was filled with daylight.

He pushed up his sleeve to check his arm.
Something etched there made him smile,
feel ready for anything.
It was a silvery morning here,
it was going to be a golden day.
He watched the birds again for a moment
against the piece of sky.
Then he sat up, looked around, smiled
and swung his mud-covered joggers to the floor.

2
Mugged

The blow sent her flying. She hit the grass with force and lay there surprised, for a moment speechless.

The old woman had not been worried to hear the thud of running feet so close behind her. She hadn't turned. She knew it would be Ben, her grandson, for sure.

Out of school this time of the afternoon, he often joined her on her daily walk across the park. She'd hear his feet, allow him to surprise her, and then a hand would slip inside hers.

'Hello, Gran. It's me!'

'Fancy that!' she'd say. 'And just what are you doing in the park?'

'Going on a walk with you.'

And if there'd been left-over bread that day he'd swing the plastic packet to show her. They'd go down to the edge of the big pond to feed the ducks.

So she didn't turn when she heard the thud of feet directly behind her. And she was totally unprepared for the impact of a blow. It sent her stumbling a few steps before she fell to the ground. Her head hit the grass with such force her glasses were sent spinning, to shatter against the stone base of a park bench.

'Oops—sorry, lady.' It was the voice of a child maybe as young as Ben.

She saw an anxious young face bending down to her.

'Don't speak to her, ya bleedin' idiot! Just grab the bag.'

This voice was older sounding. Harsh. And this voice was connected to the hard hands that held her face down on the grassy track.

'And don't say sorry, nerd. Never! Christ, kid, get it! I can't sit on her forever.'

'A couple of kids!' she thought, and raised her face indignantly. 'A couple of kids!' She found her voice.

'Get off! There's no bag. No money—nothing! Let go of me now!' She spoke with a lack of fear that set the big boy, the one who seemed in charge, back a moment.

'Shut up, Grannie!'

'Hasn't got a bag,' the young boy spoke urgently. 'Didn't you hear her? Any minute she'll start yelling.'

'Give us some money, lady,' the older voice asked, but it was less certain now.

'I won't start yelling,' she told them, 'so you can just let go of me.'

'Silly cow! Hasn't got anything anyway. C'mon!' He let her go and the two darted away into the bushes.

She looked up to see them scuttle out of sight.

'I've just been mugged,' she thought, sitting up and then gathering the remains of her glasses, 'that's what!'

She climbed to her feet, smoothing her dress and brushing grass from her skirt and hair. That was when she suddenly felt weak.

'And no one in sight. Not a soul!' She glanced around her. 'Wouldn't you know it?' she said to herself.

She sat on the park bench for a moment, inspecting her arm where there might be a bruise later. 'Shouldn't have taken a lonely path through the park. Serves me right.'

She felt helpless. The fall had shaken her up, that's all. OK, she was scared too. But not of the younger boy, the only one she'd seen properly. He looked so like Ben or his friends. Maybe a bit older. And the way he'd spoken to her. She could almost smile remembering his 'Oops—sorry, lady' when her glasses had broken against the bench. Apologising, as they pushed her to the ground to rob her!

But suddenly sitting there alone on the park bench, her shattered glasses on her lap, she found sobs rising in her throat. 'Ridiculous,' she told herself, 'you're all right. You're quite all right, Mrs Iris Walker.'

She often spoke to herself in this way, a result of living alone for so long before coming to live with her daughter and grandson.

'You've had a little fall, that's all! A bit of a shake-up and a fall. And you're quite OK. Nothing much happened, so just get to your feet and go home.' She mopped up her tears.

But the thought of home and the explanations she'd have to make to Jane made her feel tired and she lingered.

When she felt she had the strength to face her daughter, she walked slowly home, still feeling shaky.

'Just like an old lady,' she thought, quite surprised.

3
Fear

'Shut yer face will you?' Pale was annoyed to see that Robbie was crying.

He'd said they should get out of the park pretty quick after the mess up with the old lady. 'Before she goes blabbing we robbed her or something.'

But just as they'd left the bushes two police officers had come strolling down the path under the palm trees towards them.

'Pigs, what d'ya know?' Pale had muttered and stopped dead. When he turned back Robbie had followed. They'd dived back into the shelter of the thick grasses where they sat waiting, Robbie quivering in fear.

'It's dead easy to rumble someone,' Pale had explained during the long day at the park, 'long as you choose the right one. Long as there's two of you. Dead easy.'

But Robbie hadn't liked what had happened with that

old lady. Up close to her it hadn't been easy at all. His heart wasn't in it.

And Pale knew it. 'You'll be next to bleedin' useless if you go on like this,' he'd whispered as the police passed by, 'and you'll be fair game for the jacks, for sure. Get tough or get goin'.'

Robbie couldn't get going. Right now he felt nothing but fear: fear of his companion, of the police, of the court. Fear of the home and of foster parents. Fear of all this and of the feeling in his stomach right now. Hunger!

All at once, hiding in the tangle of grass, it had seemed hopeless being here with Pale. Or up at the Cross where he'd gone this morning, or anywhere. Just hopeless! But there was nowhere else for him to go. With the slow setting of the sun he'd begun to cry. When Pale had spoken sharply like that, 'Shut yer face, will you!' though, he'd stopped pretty well straight away. Pale might be thin but he was wiry and strong, and he could punch. Robbie had only known him for a day but already he'd seen his mood change ten or more times. Over-friendly and helpful one minute, to out-and-out cruel and bullying the next. Brandishing his flick knife and calling it his friend.

'You want to eat. You said so. Well, here comes an old bag. Look at her waddling along. All by herself, too. Sure to have some money. Dead easy.' Then when he saw Robbie frown, 'We don't have to hurt her real bad or anything. Just a little surprise. That's all.'

Robbie hadn't known how to get away so he'd gone

along with it.

'Look Robbie, we'll get something going tomorrow, OK?' Pale was talking, friendly now that the police were out of sight. He was feeling comfortable again. 'Anyway, I got something make you sleep like a baby.'

With quick movements the older boy fashioned a bed among the tussocks, uprooting bundles of grass to make a pillow for himself. Then he stretched out on the ground, sighing as if this were a top hotel and he'd just climbed into a super-soft bed.

'Are you going to sleep?' Robbie asked, afraid of the dark gathering all around.

'That's the general idea—so why don't you?'

Robbie could get up and go right now, he supposed. Take the long walk to the squat in Darlo that girl Amanda had told him about. But maybe he wouldn't find his way there by himself in the dark. Maybe when he got there the other kids she'd spoken of wouldn't let him in anyway. Maybe it was better on the first night, his first night in the city, to stay here with the older boy. Pale looked like he'd done this kind of thing lots of times before. So maybe just for tonight. And then tomorrow he'd find Mandy—Amanda—again and he'd get away from Pale.

4
Friends

Robbie had arrived at the place called the Cross, in the heart of the city, early morning. He was scared and yet excited that he'd made it all the way on the train, no trouble. Some kids at the last place he'd been in had told him about going there to live. They'd said there was lots to do at the Cross—it was speedy, exciting! And that you have plenty of friends when you're a streetie.

He walked along the pavements in a daze. So many flashing lights and neons and girls and bouncers and it was early morning. The nights must be crazy with people here. Every few steps there was the thump of new music and the confusion of voices. Up ahead he caught a flash of the blue uniform he knew so well. The pigs'd never look for him here—all these people—but he turned aside down a lane.

He met Amanda pretty well straight off. She must be fifteen, even sixteen, he'd thought to himself when she spoke. A tall, dark-haired girl with a crinkly smile, and so friendly. She was dressed in tight blue jeans, a boy's shirt and what looked like boy's boots. She plonked down right beside him just like that.

'I'm Amanda, called Mandy,' she announced. 'You new here, kid?'

He was sitting by the El Alamein fountain where he'd been told to come, wondering if all the kids in the raggedy jeans were just visiting the place. He hadn't found the nerve to speak to any of them.

'Yeah,' he replied.

'You on your own?'

'Yeah.'

'You run away?'

'Yeah.' He didn't quite know why he trusted Amanda straight off but he did.

'Stands out like a sore thumb,' she told him.

He frowned, scared that he'd started out all wrong here, and that because of it, he'd find no friends. Or worse: that the police would spot him right off and send him back to—well, back to nowhere really. He stood up, ready to move on.

'It's OK,' she said, laughing, 'I'm not going to dob or anything. Relax. It's just you look pretty neat and clean for one thing ...'

He would have liked to spatter himself in mud to please her.

'... and you look pretty young, even for here.'

'I'm not. I'm fifteen,' he lied.

'Sure,' she said. 'I gotta go soon. But you just watch out for any rock spider latching onto you, see.'

He looked confused.

'Men around here might say they'll look after you, OK? Just say no.'

'I know all about that.' He knew all there was to know, he reckoned, about crack and speed and the Wall where the boys worked at night. And the girls too. He'd been told by some of the kids in the place he'd been put for out-of-control youth.

Kids who'd been in that place for years knew the ropes. The place he'd escaped from less than three days ago. They might know the ropes but they were still there and he was here beginning a new life. He smiled.

'Tough guy, eh?' and she laughed.

He said nothing. He wished he was a tough guy. He was dead scared and she knew it.

'Got anywhere to sleep tonight?' she asked. When he shook his head she told him about a place he could go. The squat. Exactly how to get there through a network of streets and lanes.

'Don't go there just now. There's some crazies but they're moving out. Tonight's cool but I'll be real late, kid. My friend Tessa's there, though. Tell her Mandy said you're OK,' and she squeezed his arm and left him.

'See ya tonight,' she called over her shoulder, like they were friends or she was his sister. And he was filled with pleasure and wonder that it had been so easy to find someone. The kids who'd told him had been right. This was the place to be. 'You can find friends up there easy,' they'd said.

And then Pale had turned up just a moment or two later. He'd been asked all the same questions and more.

'You hungry?' Pale finally asked.

'Yeah,' he said, although his stomach was really churning too much to be hungry.

'What's your name?' the tall thin boy asked.

'Robbie.'

'They call me Pale,' the big boy told him without any explanation. But his pale blond hair and white, white skin made it obvious.

'We've missed the drop-off up the station. Town Hall—there's this priest guy. Good tucker, not too much talk. Go there sometimes. But there're other places here,' and he jerked his head in the direction of the busy street.

'You comin' or what?'

They walked in silence. There was no place with food for them, Robbie noticed, though they passed a succession of restaurants. The sharp smell from a pizza place was agonisingly good. Robbie stopped in the doorway to inhale it.

'You got money?' Pale asked.

'No.'

'Told you I'd get us some food and things. I'm going down the park now,' he explained. 'Come, if you want.'

The big boy loped off. Should he go or stay? The streets seemed so busy with people walking every whichway. All busy and going somewhere. It was still early morning, Robbie reminded himself. It would help fill in the day to go with Pale to the park. And he'd said about the food.

Pale seemed to want to take Robbie under his wing right from the start. 'You need to get tough round here,' Pale had explained as they walked together down the long city street that led to the big stone park gates.

'I can show you a thing or two. It's good round here but. Plenty of chicks if you want. Plenty of action. You get hyped on the streets and then you won't want to be nowhere else.'

5

Pale

Maybe he'd got tougher already, Robbie thought. He placed his head on the grass pillow he'd fashioned for himself, copying Pale. Mugging someone in broad daylight. But he knew he didn't want to do that again. No way. He was desperately afraid of getting caught and being taken back there.

He didn't like being with Pale too much, he'd decided. The big boy was trouble for sure. He didn't like the way he'd talked about things, all the girls he knew, in that funny way. And how he and a friend who was a real tough guy had bashed into some old drunk the other night. 'Nothing serious. Just fun.'

He didn't like this feeling of weakness, either. Despite Pale's boasting there'd been no food. Two long drinks at the bubblers in the park. Then a bit of snooping in the bins, quite unsuccessful and smelly. And now a pain in his gut that he hadn't felt since he'd stayed out once, slept under a bridge for two nights after the last big bust up with his father.

'I was going back to see Amanda,' he told Pale, wiping away any trace of tears in the dark. 'Do you know Amanda with the dark curly hair?'

'Sure—everyone knows Mandy,' and he laughed. 'She's wild. And she's been round this dump for yonks.'

'I like her,' he said as if to tell himself.

'Shouldn't like no one. No way,' Pale said, rolling over on his stomach and looking down on Robbie so that he finally sat up.

'Rule number one, OK? You shouldn't like no one.'

'What about a dog?' Robbie asked hopefully and Pale was silent, considering for a moment.

'Maybe animals,' he said, plucking a piece of grass and chewing on it. 'Yeah cats maybe.' Then he spat the grass. 'Nah—animals don't count,' he said, 'not really. Animals can't give you any damn thing, can they?'

But Pale rolled back restlessly onto his grass bed. He thought of a cat and a kitten he knew well and remembered a dog he'd liked once. Liked a lot too. An afternoon on the lawn at the Home when the labrador Jess had had pups.

Tom at the makeshift kennel had said, 'Come and look here, Pete,' and he'd said no because he'd felt angry with everyone, with the world. And then Tom had come across the lawn where he lay sprawled, staring up at the sky. He'd emptied two, then three small, quivering, nosy, live things right beside him. One of them with a floppy ear had licked and licked his hand and then his cheek in a frenzy of joy.

And he'd finally sat up and taken this one up in his arms and held it to him, right against his shirt.

'You can look after that little one if you want,' Tom had told him.

'Nah—don't wanna,' he'd said, putting the puppy down on the lawn again and sauntering off inside. He made sure he didn't look back. Not once.

But later that afternoon he'd gone back to the kennel. And he'd found his little puppy sniffing around at the grass outside.

'Coffee Beans,' he'd said, stroking the floppy brown ears and the fat little body and allowing the puppy caresses. 'That's who you are, mate. Coffee Beans.'

He was there night and morning after that. And when the other puppies went off to new homes Tom had allowed Coffee Beans to stay. Pale had carried him everywhere, until Coffee Beans became too indignant and too big for that. And then Coffee Beans had followed Pale everywhere.

Coffee Beans had cried piteously the day Pale had been moved to the new Home because of the fight, the knife fight with Shane. Shane had had to go to the hospital and he'd been moved out to another place in the country. It wasn't so much a Home, more a gaol, although it wasn't called that. But there were bars everywhere and screws everywhere who kept you tabbed. Tom had promised Pale he'd do everything he

21

could to get Coffee Beans moved to where Pale had been sent. But it had been impossible.

He'd kind of gone crazy in the first few weeks in the new place. And no one there wanted to do him any favours, he knew that. He'd bashed and been bashed, raved and been raved at, cried and been jeered at. Then he'd gone quiet as he could, and mean as he could too. At first he thought about Coffee Beans a lot when he was locked up alone after another fight. Then he decided to stop thinking about the dog. To stop thinking about anything nice. To get as tough as all the other bastards here. Tougher.

'Nah—animals—they catch you like keys.'

Robbie jumped when he spoke, Pale had been quiet for so long.

'Keys?'

'Yeah, and gates and things. You know, letterboxes and doors.'

'No.'

'Houses, you der! They catch you and hold you down to things. I don't want to be in no house with a door and keys for keeping people in—no way. And I don't want people liking me. Never. And I don't want to like people. It's stupid, see.'

Robbie said nothing.

'So, never like anyone. Rule number one, OK?'

Robbie knew he couldn't say no to Pale so he said, 'OK.' But he thought: Sure, Pale, I won't say to you I like anybody—I'll just like them. And I like Mandy.

I like lots of people, he thought, lying back on the tussocks dazed by the pills Pale had pulled out of his shirt pocket and given him. 'Happy-time pills, little boy—you'll sleep so sound you could piss yourself,' and he'd laughed the grating sound that he was sure would make Rob afraid.

'It's too late to get to any squat, kid. I'm too tired. So get it down and shut your trap.'

After the pills the tussocks had seemed soft and bendy and the pain in his gut subsided. He was able to think of lots of people he liked as he lay there with Pale already fast asleep beside him.

His sister, Melanie, for one. He didn't know where she was now. But when he got into the swing of things here, he'd find out for sure. She was a good kid and he liked her lots of course, even though she'd never learned to talk much. Nan had tried and tried to teach her. 'Nan-nan' was the only word she seemed to manage, mostly when the front door slammed, shaking the house, and they heard those heavy lurching steps. Their father.

And Paul, a boy he'd met in one of the Homes. Paul had thick glasses and all the jokes. He was a good kid. Robbie had even told him a bit about his dad.

'I've got a job to get,' his father had yelled at him when his nan had been sent to the hospital, seriously ill. 'So you can't stay here. You and the little kid are a bleedin' handful. And don't look at me with that hangdog look. I'll come and get you when your nan comes back, when I'm good and ready.'

But he hadn't. Not that Robbie cared whether he saw his father or not. It was a relief being away from those raging outbursts of his.

Melanie, being little and cute though she couldn't talk, had been fostered straight away. But he'd been left behind in the Home for more than a year. One day he'd heard the bad news about his nan—the news he'd always feared—officially. That was when all his hope had seemed to die. And then he'd been told about a new place he could go and the foster mother had arrived to take him.

He didn't want to think too much about what had happened there. The silly cow telling him on his first night there he was the most difficult kid she'd ever had. All because he wouldn't eat that muck she'd served on the plate. And all the fights that followed.

He'd tried those first few days, those first few weeks, to please her. Even eating the food in the end. He really had. But nothing had worked. It had been downhill all the way, with her doing her lolly and belting into him and dobbing him in for jigging school. He thought about the spray can and what he'd written right across her front door so all the world could see. He'd run away but they'd caught him every time and they'd put him in a place that was worse than hers. He'd got out of there within three days though, hadn't he? Well they'd put him in the low security wing on account of being younger. But a boy there had told him about asking to do farm work—and how you could nick off pretty simple. He'd done exactly what the boy had told him. It had seemed almost too easy. And then he'd come straight here.

And now he was lying in the park thinking of people he liked. Yeah, that was what he was doing. Melanie and poor old Paul with the stutter. And his grandmother of course. Most of all his nan. His mother, too, if he could remember her. But what was the use? He couldn't really.

Oh yeah, and he'd liked a teacher once a real lot. The teacher at Campbelltown Primary, where he'd gone to school for a while, who'd read stories and poetry and had told him he had great ideas when he'd written some things for her. He'd shown some of those things he'd written to his nan and she'd read them out loud lots of times and told him he was extra clever.

He counted them on his fingers. Yeah, three, four people he'd liked and now there was Amanda called Mandy. He was sure to like her a lot when he ran into her again. He was feeling very, very tired now. Something made him afraid to close his eyes, though. A ridiculous thought that the grass tussocks would reach down and cover him, suffocate him. But finally his eyelids drooped against his will.

And then he saw her. Coming back from the duck pond with a trail of birds following her, her nice kind face and the sun shining on her glasses. A nice old face like his nan's. He could see her turning down the little track by the seat singing to herself. And then her nice old face twisted in pain and surprise as Pale lunged at her punching, her to the ground, grabbing her arm and holding her there.

It was funny, silly, but he thought from the way she talked, pretty tough really for an old lady, that he would probably like her too.

He'd have to get away from Pale soon, he thought when his eyes opened on grass, sky and Pale's back next morning. But Pale said as he got to his feet, 'Wanna show you something. Other side of the park. Spooky as hell. And after that—breakfast for sure.'

Robbie didn't know how to say no.

6
Police

'They should be put away!' Jane was indignant. 'That's what, Mum! How on earth can you feel any sympathy for kids who'd rob you in broad daylight and hit you! A woman of your age! Anyone! I don't know!'

Iris Walker had reported the incident in such a matter-of-fact voice to the police officers that her daughter was annoyed.

'Tell them how viciously the big one punched you, Mum. You can see the bruise on her temple and one on her arm.'

'The bruise on my temple is from a rock. Not from any punch, Jane. It wasn't so much a punch that sent me flying. More a shove in the middle of my back, really. Took me by surprise, which was their idea. And down I went and this little fella—he must be new at this sort of thing—this little fella apologised straight off. Can you believe it? Hitting me and then saying sorry!' She laughed a light laugh that brought a frown to Jane's brow.

'Can you describe him?' The more senior officer began the questioning, her pen poised above the notebook in her lap.

'Just like Ben over there. Just like my grandson. Well, rather like him, I mean. A bit older.'

Iris indicated her grandson, who was pressed against the wall near the door hoping his mother wouldn't notice him. Intrigued and horrified by his grandmother's story of the mugging just across the road in the park, he wanted to hear everything.

'About thirteen?'

'Surely not,' Jane had burst out. 'A thirteen-year-old doing something like that! He must've been older, Mum.'

'Well, yes. Maybe a year older.'

'So thirteen—fourteen?' the officer asked.

'Yes—I'd say. But quite small. That could make him look younger, I suppose.'

'Dark hair and dark eyes—like your grandson?'

'Yes—but more well ...'

'Yes?'

'More foreign-looking, if you know what I mean. Greek or Lebanese I'd say. Pretty, dark eyes and such long lashes.'

'Mum!' Jane sounded disgusted. 'How can you call a little thug pretty?'

'It's just that the little one bent down so close to me, I couldn't help noticing.'

'So, an ethnic kid?'

'Well, if that's what you want to call him, yes, an ethnic kid.'

'Any distinguishing features? Scars, tattoos, that kind of thing?'

'No,' the old lady paused. 'I mean, yes, there was something ...'

'What was that, Ma'am?'

'His hands—the boy's hands. They were just like my Mark's when he was young.'

'What do you mean, Mum?' Jane sounded edgy and embarrassed.

'Musician's hands, you know.' The old woman smiled.

'Musician's?' the pen poised.

'I noticed how long and fine his hands were. Like my son's. He played piano wonderfully well even as a young boy, my son. Such long, fine hands Mark had.'

'Oh, I see,' the officer wrote deliberately.

'Anything else, Ma'am?'

'He looked tired,' she mused as if to herself, 'and he'd been crying.'

'Uh huh.'

'And I knew he didn't want to do what he was doing. His heart wasn't in it, that little kid—that's for certain.'

'Uh huh.'

The second officer, a serious young man, leaned forward now. 'And the older youth—can you describe him?'

'The one holding me down? Well—I didn't exactly get a good look at him. I heard him all right, though.'

'What age would you say he was?'

'Oh he was older, all right—sixteen or more I'd say, and tough. Well, tougher. He was after money and he was angry there wasn't any. You know, I think the young boy made him nervous. I think if the younger boy hadn't been there—then he'd have been nastier.'

'If he was like that gang I read about beating up people on the trains, he would have, Mum,' Jane interrupted. 'Probably would've bashed you senseless.'

'Oh, I don't know, Jane—but he'd have swung a few punches, probably.'

'He had blond hair, the big boy. And when I say blond I mean almost white. I remember the shock of his white hair in the sun. When they were running away into the bushes. Unusual hair.'

'Any further description of either of them—clothing?

'They ran off so quickly when they left me—I can't remember. Jeans I think. Yes, jeans. A bit like Ben here. A bit like every other kid out and about—you know. And those jogger shoes—a bit tatty-looking. I'm sorry I can't be more helpful.'

'You've been very helpful,' the younger officer told her. 'It's a gang, I think. One's been doing the park and the shopping centre these last few days. Streeties after money for drugs, more than likely.'

'Streeties?'

'Homeless kids. Their beat is generally up at the

Cross. But there's a gang drifting round Paddington at present. Bag snatching—that sort of thing. Some of these kids have taken to sleeping out in the park.'

'Are there many of these streeties?'

'Yes, Ma'am. More and more.'

'Shameful really. A child without a home.'

'You're right, Mum, it's shameful,' Jane interrupted,' but that's the way it is these days. And sad or not, it doesn't give them the right to——'

'I've read about them, of course. But who are they, these kids?' the old woman asked.

'Runaways, strays. You get all types up there these days.'

'And there's really nowhere for them to go?'

Jane cut in. 'Mum used to foster kids quite a few years ago. That was in her own home in Lismore. And they were country kids.'

'Lots of success stories,' Mrs Walker told the officers, 'and a few failures, I'd have to admit. But at least there were places for kids to go. Not the streets!'

'Well, there's shelters and the church places—various agencies provide homes. But not enough for all of them. There're a lot of kids out there, Ma'am. You'd be surprised.'

'They could get back to their families,' Jane interrupted. 'That's what they could do. And stop preying on people like us.'

'Not always possible I'm afraid, Ma'am,' the young officer began. 'For a start, some of them don't have parents or a family to speak of ...'

'Well, you should stop them interfering in decent-living people's lives. They have all the making of thugs and criminals, kids who get away with goings-on like this!'

Ben thought he had never seen his mother more angry, but his grandmother didn't seem angry at all.

'Oh, I think the little fella was probably OK at heart,' the old woman said to her daughter. 'Probably never had a chance.'

'Chance or not, he's a thief, Mum. Or a would-be thief—probably violent if it came to it.'

'The younger ones aren't generally violent, Ma'am. It's the older kids—they can be more of a problem.'

'A problem! I know what I'd like to do with them,' Jane said fiercely. 'And I wouldn't muck about!' She glared at the police officers as if they were slacking on the job right then and there.

'Sounds a bit like that Wallace kid to me, you know,' the young man spoke to the other officer. 'The kid with white hair,' and then to Iris: 'Might get you to come and look at some mug shots. Maybe tomorrow if you'd be so kind, Mrs Walker.'

They both stood to go. 'May we suggest to you that you don't go strolling in the park alone?' the young man said.

'She certainly won't,' Jane replied. Ben, still quiet as a mouse against the wall, thought it was funny to hear his mother talking about Gran as if she were a child.

He glanced at Gran but she was smiling at the officers. 'Thank you for that advice.'

Jane saw them out and they could hear her indignant voice all the way up the hall. 'The kind of kids who do this sort of thing ... Something surely has to be done ...'

'Gran, are you walking in the park ever again?' Ben asked after tea when his mother had left the room.

'I should think so, Ben. But not on that lonely path I took today. I'd be too scared to go that way again—and it was silly I suppose. I'll go down the main road. Plenty of people about there. And you're not to worry ...'

'What about the younger boy—the boy like me? What if he's there? And the big boy?'

'The boy like you is a very frightened boy, Ben. I don't think he'll do anything to harm me. In fact I'm sure of it. And the police seem to know the other boy. They'll probably pick him up in no time.'

'Well, I'm coming with you if you go,' Ben said, and I'm bringing a big stick.'

When his mother joined them Ben asked, not for the first time that week, 'When's Dad coming back, Mum?'

He didn't like the idea of the big boy with white hair in the park, just across the road from their house. His father had been away overseas for ages and ages. Sometimes he thought his dad might never come back.

'I've told you before, Ben, I don't know. Soon, I expect,' his mother said in an annoyed voice which made both Ben and his grandmother very quiet.

As Iris was leaving to go to her flat at the back of the house, Jane had one more go at her. 'These city kids are not like the kids you used to look after, Mum. Times have changed and kids have changed, so don't go and get any silly ideas. They're too far gone, these street kids. Hard bitten. No good! Wild things. Beyond help most of them, believe me!'

In her bed, Iris cried briefly for the second time that day. She'd helped lots of troubled kids in her time. Knew exactly how to talk to them, to give order to their disordered lives, to give love to them, lots of it, and then watch the miracle as they blossomed into 'ordinary' kids.

She wasn't a social worker or a police officer but she reckoned she knew as much about wild kids as anyone needed to know. She'd known a few beauties! And given a chance she'd be helping now if only her heart hadn't acted up the way it did. No matter what Jane said, she didn't believe—couldn't believe—that a kid as young as that boy in the park, a kid with that face, could be beyond help.

She cried too, thinking about how hard it was going to be to face the park. She was frightened about going there alone now but she knew she must go. It was like after the car accident. You had to make yourself get in the car and drive.

Well, she'd make herself go to the gate of the park and walk nice and slowly down the main road and the main path. No more sidetracks.

She'd go tomorrow or she might never go again. And the park over there, with its trees and gardens, with its ducks and birds, was the only thing keeping her sane in this big lonely city.

After she'd placated Ben's fears of the bad boys, Jane didn't feel at all like sleeping. Stories about violent gangs of youths in shopping malls and on the streets seemed to be getting more and more frequent these days. And with this happening so close to home ... She knew she'd been sharp with her mother when the police had come, and unforgiving about the boy, but fear had made her angry.

Jane went to the cocktail cabinet and poured herself a long drink. She switched on the television, but though she sat there, she didn't really watch it. She was lost in thought. Yes, she mused, with her husband Paul so far away now, having her mother come to live close by had seemed such a good idea, all those months ago. But there were problems. Her mother could do things, with good intentions of course, that were so thoughtless. She'd brought that injured possum home from the park the first week she'd moved in. And then there'd been such a to-do with Ben when he'd discovered he wouldn't be allowed to keep it forever. And taking the back path through the park today to look at the water lilies, when she'd been expressly told why she shouldn't. Plain silly! But there was something else about having her mother so closely enmeshed in their lives, something Jane hadn't anticipated at all. She had to face it, she thought now, slowly sipping her drink. She was more than a touch jealous of the affection Ben so readily gave to his grandmother, and she knew that wasn't fair.

She'd try to discuss things more sensibly tomorrow. Try to get on better with her mother all round. But it was going to be difficult. Jane sat alone in the large lounge room and drank quite a bit more wine before she finally felt sleepy enough to make her way to bed.

7

Underground

'It's a huge bleedin' tank,' Pale explained, 'right under this grass. You know, a place to hold water. Soddin' mountains of it too!'

They'd walked to the very edge of the park, over the longish grass still thick with dew, and climbed inside another fence that enclosed a circle of clipped lawn.

It looked like a sports oval to Robbie until Pale showed him the holes. Round, fat holes in the green lawn, covered with metal.

Pale prised one of them open. 'Yahoooo,' he called, and his voice echoed down and down to somewhere far beneath the grass.

'And the metal posts all around the grass. You can call down them, too. Airholes. Wanna try?'

But Robbie shook his head.

'It's got water down there mostly. Except it's empty right now. And that's why we're going to take a lookie inside.'

Robbie nodded. He didn't like looking down the round shaft where Pale's voice had echoed, deep underground, so far away. And he didn't want to take a lookie inside either.

But Pale seemed very keen. 'In summer me and this little kid Ritch tied ourselves to a rope here. We let ourselves down into the place. Water's not up to the top, see. God, talk about spooky. But we had us our own private swimming pool. Bleedin' huge! Swam round in the dark whenever we wanted on hot days. Black water flapping round you.'

Robbie shuddered at the thought of the two white figures swimming in the great blackness of that tank underground. Filled with black water. The thought of the place empty was almost as bad.

'And just this bit of rope to climb out again. "If the rope broke," I used to love to say to Ritch cause he'd kind of spew then, and it was funny just watching him. "If the rope broke then you and me'd be floating round in this here place forever. Till we got too tired that is. Till we started gaggin' on the water. Till we sank under the water." Jesus, you should've seen the kid swim for the rope then!

' "No one'd ever know," I'd say, and he'd go hell for leather, that kid. He'd want to get out then and there. "We'd rot down here. Our flesh'd go soggy and start droppin' off. Turn to skeletons we would, and no one'd ever find us!" I used to yell after him. "Skeletons." God, that'd take him up the rope on the double.

'Funny little kid. Don't know what happened to him. He was around, and then he just kind of disappeared all of a sudden. So, what's new?'

Pale started across the green oval and climbed down the grassy bank.

'Maybe his skeleton's under there.' He laughed. 'We should take a look.'

'Nah, I don't really ...' Robbie began.

'C'mon. There's no skeletons, kid. Not that I saw. It's bleedin' spooky, this place, now it's empty. Should see it.'

'But all that water ...'

'It's empty, I tell you. So we can walk right through a hole they've made in the wall. Lookie round and then shoot through OK?'

Again there seemed no way out.

They trudged down a makeshift road to the high wall of the reservoir. Pale climbed the wire fence with ease and prised back the wooden covering to reveal the mouth of darkness inside.

'Told ya,' he called back over his shoulder. 'Spooky as hell, but you gotta come in. It's like the movies in here.' His voice was echoing now. 'Yeah, you could have a shoot-out with all those pillars every whichway. Or a drag race.'

Robbie hung back.

'Jesus, these walls are thick,' Pale called out to him.

Robbie didn't want to look at the thickness. Once through the hole he knew he'd be behind the walls of a fortress, one that could fill with water any old time.

A dim light came through a few of Pale's airholes way up there on the oval, but otherwise the walls and floor were shiny, dark and wet.

'It's big,' he said, because Pale expected something of him. 'Jesus, it's big!'

'You could rollerblade through here. Right through,' Pale sounded enthusiastic. 'What d'ya say?'

'I say I'm hungry.' Robbie expected Pale's anger, but the older boy laughed.

'God, you're a whinger. We'll go down the railway station then. There's a food drop-off at 8.30 on the dot. C'mon.'

But once outside in morning light, Pale stopped to look at the makeshift sign. 'Read it,' he instructed.

'Read it yourself,' Robbie said, walking past, braver now in the light of day. When he looked up though, Pale's face made him turn back to the sign.

'Nice and loud, too,' Pale said, moving away to the top of the road as if he was on the lookout for someone.

Robbie raised his voice so Pale could hear.

THIS RESERVOIR IS ONE OF THREE TO SUPPLY THE EASTERN SUBURBS AND THE CITY OF SYDNEY WITH DRINKING WATER. IT IS TEMPORARILY EMPTIED FOR A PERIOD OF THREE MONTHS FOR REPAIRS TO THE NORTHERN WALL. ERECTED IN 1894, THIS IS THE FIRST TIME IN 100 YEARS THE RESERVOIR HAS BEEN EMPTIED. SPECIAL NOTE: IT WILL BE OPENED TO THE PUBLIC FOR VIEWING FOR TWO DAYS ONLY IN MAY.

*STRICTLY OUT OF BOUNDS WITHOUT A SYDNEY
WATER BOARD REPRESENTATIVE.*
COUNCIL OF THE CITY OF SYDNEY

'That's what I thought it said,' Pale muttered when
Robbie joined him.

8
Dreaming

She dreamed of home that night ... of being young again, on the river with George and Mark and Jane in the old rowboat.

The faces of her husband and children were so vivid and the water so green! The ordinary beauty of the country morning on the river astounding her as it always had.

Mark was rocking the boat from side to side and she was laughing.

It was pleasant waking with the thought of their faces. But then there were slashes of light through venetian blinds. And this was now and she was old, not young and laughing on the river. Her husband was dead. She was living at the back of her daughter's large house in a neat little flat with its view of a neat clipped lawn. She was here, close to the only family she now had, awakening to another long day.

Staring out at the tree by the window Iris thought that ever since she'd arrived here in Sydney she hadn't much liked to wake up. Back home on the Clarence River there had always been the tumult of waking. The river rushing, trees sighing in the wind, the clatter of birds. And things to look forward to, looking out her kitchen window. Oh, it had been terrible leaving the old house, perched in its tangly garden so close to the wild river.

But after her illness, Jane had insisted that she move to Sydney to be near them. Jane had said she should sell the old house too.

'No one will buy this old bag of bones,' Iris had told her daughter, 'now it has only a garden and no parcel of land to go with it.' And she'd been right. Nobody had so much as looked.

'Well, we'll have to come back some time and do it up and have another go at selling,' Jane had said.

She'd felt mean deserting the old house. Leaving it to rot among hibiscus and sugar-cane fields. Walking out on all her happy memories there: her childhood, close by; she and George buying the house; bringing up the children; all the happy times on the river.

'You can live in the flat at the back of us, Mum. At least we're close to doctors and hospital, and I can keep an eye on you. You can have your own life, of course,' Jane had said.

Her own life. But what of her own life? There didn't seem much of a life away from the birds and her garden and the great arm of the river. It comforted her to think of her furniture, most of it too big or too old, according to Jane, to bring. It was still in place there in the silent house. There, waiting, as if she could go back any time. Not that Jane would let her, now. Thank God for Ben and for the park!

She thought about the nameless younger boy in the park as she rose to put the kettle on the stove. 'Homeless,' the police officers had said. It seemed incredible that a child as young as he was should be without a home.

She thought of him all the morning. She hoped that she would see him again. Maybe in some small way she might be able to help him.

9

Bondi Beach

'You got to do it, see,' Pale told Rob, 'you're small and frizzy haired. All those bleedin' curls all over. And you look like butter wouldn't melt ... You gotta be the one to go in first. They'll trust you, see.'

'I told you I don't want ...'

'Listen, you gotta get tough, kid. If you're going to be a streetie then you better act like one. If you stick round me I'll teach you things. I told you I know the places to sleep. I know where you can get a feed. I know places where it's easy to pinch stuff. And I can get you some good dope—speed, crack, you name it. Now stay if you want, or piss off now.'

Robbie said nothing

'OK then, you coming with me?'

'Yeah.' Pale knew he was frightened. Too frightened to say no, anyway.

'Easy as taking candy from a baby,' the big boy said. 'It's an art gallery in there. Pictures every-sodding-where. 'You go in ahead of me, you'll see what I mean. I been in there once and there's this woman sitting at a table, see. The thing is to get her away from the table. That's the plan. You go in and look at the painting, real slow. And while you're looking, take a gecko at the side door. Cause that's where we get out. Jump down onto the promenade and up the sewer pipe. Easy, see? You take a real slow look at the paintings, but don't look at the ghetto blaster. It'll be at her feet. It's a beauty and it'll buy us more than dinner, OK?

" So I come in and do my stuff. You grab the ghetto blaster and by then I'll've opened the door and out we go. Simple as that. And don't look so bleedin' lost. OK? You go in there and look real happy to see those paintings all over the wall. You look real interested and keep your eyes off the ghetto blaster till the last minute.'

Robbie didn't like the way Pale was keeping the finger on him. Had stopped him twice now from getting back to look for Mandy. And he kept pestering him to do things he didn't want to do.

He'd been chased out of the corner store when Pale made him steal the potato chips out of a big stand right at the front. He'd told Pale it was a stupid idea right at the front like that, so obvious. He'd dropped the lot, he'd been so frightened by the yelling and by the sight of two big guys lunging round the counter. They'd chased him halfway up Bondi Road.

He'd ducked into a big supermarket and managed to hide in the refrigerated room, otherwise they'd have caught him, for sure. And by the look of them they'd have beaten the daylights out of him. He didn't care about stealing the chips. He'd shoplifted before; chocolates and a shirt once and some flower pots. He hadn't known what he could do with the flower pots, though, and he'd left them down a lane. But this stuff Pale did—this was crazy!

Pale had thought the chase down Bondi Road was fun. 'Should've seen those jerks run. One with a big fat gut too. And you looked a real gook.'

'Ah, shut up, Pale,' he'd said, but Pale wouldn't shut up. He went over and over it all the way to the beach.

'I'll say this—you're fast. God, did you move!' and he burst out laughing again.

Robbie was tired from the night of broken sleep, and hunger. Little fingers of pain were clawing at his gut and the spit kept forming in his mouth when he thought of food. Lashings of steaming fettuccine in a bowl, like his grandmother had made, with thick bolognaise sauce. He could just about faint at the thought of it. Pale had come good with a can of Coke he'd nicked from a fruit shop fridge and some chocolate, but there was still this awful feeling of emptiness.

He'd do this thing in the art gallery at Bondi Beach with Pale. After that, when he had some food in his stomach, then he'd feel a whole lot better, then he'd make a plan. He'd go somewhere else, find Mandy or someone else. Get away from Pale, today.

'You got it?' Pale went over the plan again in minute detail.

'Yeah,' Robbie strode up the promenade that ran the full length of the beach, right to the door of a graceful arched building called the Pavilion.

'Turn left inside the door,' Pale had told him. 'There's double doors wide open. Go inside and act cool. Just look interested. Cool, see, and move all round the place slowly. Like you've got a big fat wallet stuffed with money and you're gonna buy the whole lot!'

He felt awkward as he came through the doors. There was a couple whispering in one corner of the large room, and at a table against the back wall a young woman sat, watching. Just like Pale had told him, there was the ghetto blaster right at her feet. There was some kind of posh music playing. He could swoop across the room when Pale came in and grab it. Easy. Like Pale said, taking candy from a baby. For a minute, with his heart thumping just a bit noisily, he felt a thrill of excitement as he prepared himself. Can I do it? Can I grab the thing before she squawks the place down?

Then he felt her eyes on him and there was that quiet voice, 'You like looking at the paintings, do you?'

'Don't talk to her,' Pale had said. 'Don't eyeball her. Just circle the room slowly, slowly. And make sure you're close to the table when I come in.'

'Mmf,' he made a kind of strangled response. Then he moved as far away from the dark-haired woman as he could.

'C'mon, Pale, where the hell are you?' He was moving too fast round the room now. Great swirls and stripes of colour dazzled him. He dared not take them in but concentrated on the bare walls in between. Seven, eight, nine, ten. 'Count to twenty and I'll be there.'

He was counting too fast, wasn't he? Too damn fast.

OK—again—again. Seven ... eight ... nine ... ten ... He'd moved past the couple and past the table and past the double door. Oh hell, was he going to get around the room again by the time Pale arrived? He'd be too far from the ghetto blaster to nick it. Slow down, idiot! Slow right down.

He was halfway round for the second time when Pale bounded in the door. Even Robbie was unprepared for what Pale did, for his performance.

He seemed to leap through the air into the middle of the gallery space, letting out a blood-curdling shriek as he went. The couple in the corner didn't wait to see what happened next—they made straight for the double doors.

Another unearthly cry came out of Pale's mouth. The woman had left the table and she was standing between Pale and the doors.

'You'll have to leave,' she was saying nervously, 'You'll have to leave at once. Come on now. Stop all that.'

'*Aaaeeeeh*.' The cry was unnerving and Robbie felt the woman's fear. Felt she wanted to run for the door

49

too, but she was gutsy. She stood her ground.

'Stop it,' she demanded, her face flushed, sounding like a school teacher. 'And get out of here. Now! Get out! Or I'll call the guard.'

Pale swirled and twirled in mad circles. 'Make me go. Make me. Make me,' he goaded her. He was drawing her away from the table with his grinning mouth and his taunting words. Away and away, and this was Robbie's moment, the moment to swoop in and grab the ghetto blaster. To follow Pale across the big empty space of the room, right to where he'd said he would wrench back the large bolt on the side door. And then they could spill out onto the promenade laughing with the drama of it. They could disappear into the sewer outlet before she had time to get any guard.

But he hesitated for a moment. What if the bolt on the door didn't move back? They'd be caught like animals in a trap. He'd be caught with the thing in his hands.

Robbie's hesitation enraged Pale, still dancing in the middle of the gallery. 'Grab it, dogbreath,' he yelled. 'Go on. Grab it!'

His cry sent Robbie spinning into action. He dived across the room, but now the woman could see what was about to happen. She made a lunge for the player at the same time, and their heads almost collided.

But Robbie was an instant ahead of her—he had it. Oh God, he had the ghetto blaster! When he turned towards the side door, daylight dazzled him. Pale, as good as his word, had sped across the room and wrenched it open. There was the escape, like he'd said, the way out and no problem.

'Move it!' Pale bellowed and he ran, ducking past the woman easily and out into the fierce, bright light. He could see Pale ahead and he followed, fast as he'd ever run, breathlessly fast. Cries of people behind them. Her voice screaming something. Oh, he ran fast! Pale had disappeared now. He leapt down onto the sand and there was Pale motioning him like some crazed traffic cop. Motioning him into the outlet tunnel. He dived in and Pale followed.

Running up into the dark of the sewer outlet clutching the ghetto blaster, he felt safe. He felt clever. They'd done it! He'd done it! God, it was great to be in here and so far up the tunnel and safe! He laughed along with Pale in sheer relief and the echo of their laughter swirled round them in the confined space like a madness in the air.

He laughed because the plan had worked so easily. He laughed knowing that Pale could get money now and tonight they could eat. Pizzas and doner kebabs, any old thing they wanted. And Pale would have his tinnies and his dope, whatever!

'Better get further up,' Pale gasped when their laughter had finally subsided to weak giggles. He plucked the ghetto blaster from Robbie. 'The pigs won't usually come this far up here.'

'Aren't we safe now?'

The tunnel narrowed just a few metres ahead and here

it disgorged a slow, bright green slime.

'C'mon, get down and get going.'

But Robbie stood there, uncertain, until Pale kicked him so hard behind the knees that he fell forward onto all fours.

'C'mon. I said get going.' There was no laughter in Pale's voice any more.

'It's full of muck,' Robbie said at the entrance, fearing the slimy wet walls and the evil-smelling darkness up ahead.

'Crawl,' Pale commanded, and another kick sent Robbie head first into the muck.

'Crawl,' the voice would croak at him whenever he stopped, and in the filthy blackness he went on in fear.

Pale would not release him from that vile tunnel until it was night. They emerged and padded over the beach. The white glitter of the sand and the surf in the moonlight was almost unbearably bright.

'God, you look a sight!' Pale giggled. 'A bleedin' mess.'

It was true. Robbie's face was smeared with muck and his jeans were daubed with thick black sludge.

'Just as well you've got that hotel room with the hot shower,' Pale said. 'Well, see ya. I'm going to get changed. And I gotta see someone. You can find me tomorrow round the Cross somewhere. Late.'

And still clutching the ghetto blaster he was gone, springing up onto the promenade and taking off in long loping strides.

'Hey, Pale, wait ...' but Robbie didn't try to follow. There was no use—he could see that.

10

Alone

The excitement, the elation, and then the humiliation in the sewer outlet had left Robbie exhausted. Pale might have a change of clothes somewhere but he had nothing. He trudged down to the surf, unlaced his joggers and rolled up his stinking jeans. The surf was running nicely, with deep eddying swirls of water so that, leaning over, he could immerse his whole head and rub and scrub the revolting fishy slime off his hair and face. He even rinsed his mouth, enjoying the clean, salty taste.

He'd like to go in for a swim. He *would* go in. It must be well after midnight but who cares, he thought. The beach was empty. Who would see him, a small figure naked in the surf? He laid out his clothes carefully, wishing there was some way he could wash the filthy jeans. Then he plunged into the surf, joyous for a moment in the clean swirly mass of it. God it was cold out here in the waves! Probably sharks about too. But the surf was too inviting and he had to get the sewer smell off him.

Out beyond the breakers he looked up at a large and starry heaven with the clouds rolled back. He remembered what his nan had said about when she was a little girl and had first seen starfish. She'd cried because she thought the stars had fallen out of the sky and were scattered all over the bottom of the sea. She could hardly wait until it was night time to check if what her father said was true—that there were stars in two places. Funny how he thought about her so much, things she'd told him about her childhood, which seemed to him like a dream.

Later he knelt over the jeans, rubbing them with a terry towelling hat he'd found in a hollow in the sand, sponging and sponging away the slime and the muck. When he put them back on he thought there was only a faint smell of the sewer left.

Once again it seemed too late to go looking for the squat and Amanda. He'd have to sleep here. There was a deep doorway up at the surf lifesaving pavilion. He could curl up there out of the wind. As long as he got going early in the morning he'd be all right.

But he was wakened in what seemed like five minutes after he'd fallen asleep.

'Shouldn't you be at home, fella?'

There was a stinging torchlight in his eyes and behind the bright beam a burly security guard was bending over him.

'On your way now. No place to sleep, kid.' The voice was not unkind, but it was insistent. 'C'mon now. Get going!'

Groggy with the need for sleep, he stumbled along the promenade. Across the street a few gaudy neon lights shone. There was a milkbar that was open. But hell, he had no damn money to buy a drink or a chocolate—anything. He began the weary climb up the hill, past the houses and blocks of flats which were mostly in darkness.

He kept walking until the big park came up again. He slipped inside the open side gate. On the pathway he was startled for a moment by a bright-eyed possum ransacking a bin. There was bounty there for him, too: half a sandwich and a scarcely touched apple which he wolfed down with relish. Then he made for the exact spot where he and Pale had slept the night before and sank down in the darkness. The grass seemed like a soft and welcoming bed.

Tats

In the morning he began to make his way back towards the fountain to try to find Pale, and then Amanda. He was scared she might forget all about him if he didn't see her soon. He'd tell her he was going to the squat tonight if he could get away. He had to cut with Pale altogether, but not before he got some money out of him, the money Pale must have from the ghetto blaster by now.

He should be moving as fast as he could; on the lookout. But the thought of Pale and his cruel moods made him slow. Maybe he didn't think much of this city.

Breaking his neck to get here and now it just seemed like anywhere else—only dirtier, noisier, more frightening. And there seemed to be cops every way you looked. Not that any of them had bailed him up yet. Still it made him nervous, those cars cruising around at night. Pale had told him what to say if he were stopped. A false name and a false address and swear he was going home right away.

And the gangs. He knew which parts of town to avoid already. 'Keep your nose out of their business and they won't worry you,' Pale had said. But how, when they thought just walking past them was asking for trouble? He'd never felt as hungry as he had here either. Even when that woman had locked up the food in her kitchen because he hadn't eaten her slops.

When he came to a leafy park near a hospital, the sun on the grass looked inviting. He sat down under one of the big, old trees and felt the warmth on his body, making him sleepy. He saw that his jeans were still pretty messy and wondered listlessly where he could wash them properly. He could hear Pale's voice already, surprised and angry at such a question.

'Wash them? You must be joking. Just nick a new pair. At the markets Saturday.' Pale had already instructed him about just where you could get what round the place.

A mother had put her baby on a rug under a huge Moreton Bay fig tree nearby. God, that little thing had a loud laugh! It rolled around on the rug like a puppy. Maybe he could pretend he was on a picnic. Well, he soon would be when Pale gave him some of the money. What would he buy? A pizza—a big one he'd keep all to himself too. And chips and a thickshake and lots of chocolate.

He lay down and closed his eyes. The baby's laughter rolled over him like water. He could be by the dream river, he thought, with his nan. Running through the narrow pathways that criss-crossed the most beautiful town in the world. She'd once shown him pictures of it—a grey misty dream place with handsome domed churches and the river of glittery water. And the boats, always ready to take you anywhere you wanted. The silvery place where everyone was always happy. Oh hell! Something scratched annoyingly on his cheek. His eyes flew open as he sat up.

'Wondered where you'd got to, kid.'

It was Amanda—Mandy—looking down at him. She had a leafy twig in her hand.

'You didn't make it. And I bleedin' well kept a look-out for you, too.' She sank down beside him, pretty in her checked shirt. Her boots looked new and shiny, he noticed them straight away.

He sat up, trying to suppress the huge smile of pleasure at seeing her. He'd been so worried about ever seeing her again and here she was standing in front of him. And *she'd* found *him*. Mandy had found him! She was a friend all right.

'We slept in the big park over that way,' he waved his arm in the direction he'd come from. 'Me and this kid called Pale. Then last night ... I couldn't ... I dunno ...'

'Pale. So that's where you've been. Don't hang round with that jerk. He's bad news. Clocks onto little kids like you.'

'He's giving me some money. This arvo. He said he'd meet me.'

Mandy's laughter was not nice. A loud jeering hoot. 'Got to be kidding. Pale give you money? Pale give you anything?'

'But he said ...'

'What—he made you nick something? And he said he'd pay you later? Forget it. Every cent he gets together goes to his so-called mate, who keeps him supplied.'

Robbie stared at her.

'Crack—you der.'

'Oh.' He felt ridiculous in front of her. As if he could cry because he'd known Pale would let him down, known it all along. He couldn't remember the free food places, either, that Pale had told him were around here. Maybe you couldn't get anything now till teatime.

'You hungry?' she asked as if she'd read his mind.

'Sort of.'

They sat in a grimy, brightly lit pizza shop and she watched him eat as she took long slow sips of her Coke. He'd put away a medium-sized Pizza Supreme and was now working through a bucket of chips. He was filled to bursting point and the day didn't look so bleak any more. He thought Mandy was probably the most beautiful girl he'd ever seen, too. Her dark hair was shining in the sunlight that was bounding through the door. He noticed that her clothes were very clean too. He'd ask her about washing his jeans. She wouldn't laugh at him, he was sure.

'Go up to the City Mission. It's just round the corner. You can get a hot shower too. Only,' her face screwed up, 'you're kinda young. They don't put you in or anything, but on account of your being so young I don't know that I'd hang round there. Say you're fifteen or something if anyone asks. Anyway, how old are you?'

'Fifteen.'

'C'mon, Robbie, I'm not going to dob on you.'

'Nearly fifteen.' He took another swig of his thickshake.

'Twelve.'

'Nah—I'm thirteen.'

'Honest? You look like you could be twelve. You're just a little squirt then, aren't you?'

'Yeah.' He didn't even mind when she talked like this.

'Oh well,' she said breezily, 'who cares, eh?' She tousled his hair as if he was a really little kid.

He smiled and pushed the chips towards her, 'Want some?'

'Nah. I'm kinda sick at the moment. You know, as far as food goes.'

She didn't look sick at all.

She ran her fingers self-consciously through her hair and he noticed the flick of a tattoo on her wrist.

'What's that of?'

'My tat? Look, it's a frog.' She pulled up her sleeve. 'Cute little thing isn't it? And I've got one on my bum too. Even cuter. Can't show you that right now,' and she laughed.

'Does it hurt?' he asked. 'You know, having it done?'

'No way. Just little pinpricks, that's all. My friend Gemma does it on the cheap. She's got her own shop and all. Called Da Vinci's. Joke, eh? It's all proper but she does it for me for a good price. So I've got them on both arms up here,' and she pointed through her T-shirt to the top of her arms.

'Hey, you want a tat?'

He nodded his head. Yes, he wanted a tat. One just like hers.

'No worries,' she said taking a final swig of her Coke. 'You coming then?'

'Where?'

'To get one, silly.'

'Now?'

'Why not?'

'But I got no money.'

'And I'm flush. Got heaps right now. Let's go!'

It was hard keeping up with Mandy. She flew along the pavement, past the coffee shops and the fire station and across the big, wide, main street. Then she was off again through a maze of streets.

'It's down here,' she called over her shoulder, and there was a shopfront. One you wouldn't find easily unless you knew it—down a narrow lane off a lane off a main street.

The windows of Da Vinci's were covered with

photographs of tats. Arms and biceps, chests and torsos, stomachs, breasts, backs and backsides covered with scrolly drawings of dragons and serpents, skulls and chains, exotic animals and birds of strange plumage, naked ladies and posturing men and sentimental messages like *Narelle Forever*. Inside there were drawings covering every wall. A pile of photograph albums revealed even more designs to choose from.

'Get a little one to begin with,' Mandy told him, flicking through a large book. 'Here, what about a rabbit? You look a bit like a frightened rabbit,' and she laughed.

'I already know what I want,' he told her.

'Good one,' she said from the corner of the room, where she had settled with the book. 'Hell—take a look at this tat, why don't you?' and she was laughing so hard that he laughed before he even looked.

Gemma poked her head around a thick black curtain. 'Be with you in a sec.'

He felt a bit scared then. God, it must take hundreds of needles to get a drawing like that onto your arm to stay forever. And it must hurt a bit.

'Don't worry.' Mandy must have noticed his expression. 'It's cool. I wouldn't have brought you here otherwise. Relax.'

He proffered his arm to Gemma when she had sat him down on a chair behind the curtain.

'I want the frog, please. Just like hers,' he told her.

He watched, fascinated, as she drew the frog on his

arm with a fine pen in careful, artistic strokes.

'D'you like it?' she asked. 'I can change it if you don't. That's just an outline for me to work with. What d'you reckon?'

He nodded. 'I like it.'

'Now choose your colours, OK?'

'Amanda's is green, isn't it?'

'Sure, but you can have any colour—see these, all these here. Any colour you want.'

'I want green,' he told her.

'Well, green it is.'

She filled something that looked to Robbie like a cross between a needle and a gun. Well, more a needle really, with a thick point. And then he felt the prick, prick of the needle on his skin. It seemed like ages he was sitting there, the needle darting in and out, the stain of green ink embedded now in his skin. But Mandy said it was only forty minutes and no more when he came out from behind the curtain.

'Some take up to two hours, you know, they're that complicated,' Gemma told him.

'Look at the kid. He can't stop smiling,' Gemma laughed as Robbie proudly showed Mandy the little frog, crouched forever brightly green on his forearm.

'Spewin', mate,' she said, which he knew meant 'Fantastic!'

'You look like the cat that ate the canary,' Gemma said.

And it was true. He wanted to keep looking at it. And

while he looked he couldn't help smiling. It pleased him in a way nothing had pleased him for a long time.

But Gemma covered it with a bandaid. 'There'll be a scab for a day or two, Robbie. And then, when it falls off, the frog will be there just like now. Remember, you've got to wash it every day ...'

Mandy passed over some notes and Robbie was worried to see it was so much.

'I'll pay you back,' he told her as they left. 'Honest.'

'I got your address,' she joked. 'I'll come round to collect. So don't you try to leave town, OK?'

And pressing some notes into his pocket, she was gone, leaving him to face the streets alone.

He went up and down by the City Mission place. There was a shopfront and he could see some kids sitting on old lounges. Must be watching a TV in the back room. There were more kids drifting in the front door. He could just push that door open and go in, couldn't he? But then what if they—the people in charge in there—what if they started asking questions? What if they wanted to send him away? What if they knew he'd done a bolt from that place they'd put him? What if they called the police and there was another Home—or worse still a foster home like the last one? He walked on past it.

He'd head to the squat and rest for a while. Then he could come out at night time and have a meal and take a bit of a look around for Pale again.

12
The Squat

He'd come in through the broken, boarded-up window at the side of the old house, lifting a plank and squeezing in just like Mandy had told him. Twice now she'd given him directions. Good ones, because he found the place, no trouble. He was nervous about the other kids, the crazies who might still be there.

'Hey, hullo,' he called down a dark, dank hallway, just so they wouldn't think it was the police.

'There's only one room without leaks in it. That's where we live mostly,' Mandy had explained. 'Not the bleedin' Ritz Hotel mind you,' and she'd laughed again. 'I lived in the carpark of a posh hotel for a whole week. Once I took a bath every day in their rooftop pool. But they cottoned on, the nerds. Came in one day. New security routine and this idiot put me out. Oh well. No security jerks at the squat.'

'Hullo,' he called again, not knowing quite what to

expect in the gloom.

'Down here.' He heard a girl's voice and followed it to the end of the hall. It was dim, but he could see there were damp stains and green mossy-looking stuff all over the walls. The smell of the place was strong, horrible. Piss, he thought, and something decaying, worse.

'Get your ass in here if you're good-looking,' the girl called out, and he opened the door. When he first looked in, the room seemed empty. Well, empty except for the rubbish spread all over the floor. But then he saw her sitting on a mattress, leaning against the wall, smoking. A thin girl, extra thin he thought, with long brown hair falling softly round her shoulders, making her face seem even thinner.

'Must be Robbie?' she asked, flicking back her hair like a television ad for shampoo.

He nodded.

'C'mon in. Mandy told us you were pretty. And green! It's OK, I won't bite you. Sit. Sit,' and she flicked her hair again.

He cleared a space and sat nervously on the floor with his back against the wall.

'I'm Tessa,' she said, glancing sideways at him. 'You want some?' She passed her smoke towards him.

'Ah, no thanks.' He produced the can of cola he'd bought and drank from that.

'You an immigrant?' she asked after a pause.

'Nah.'

'Sure as hell look like a boyfriend I had once. Memhet. Or some damn name like that. What country you from?'

'Australia,' he said.

'Could've fooled me with your big cow eyes.' But she said it in a friendly way, not like the kids at school or in the Home.

'My nan came from Italy,' he told her.

'Knew you was an immigrant. Itie eh?'

'She always called me Roberto.'

'Hey, Roberto. Hey—sexy name, eh? Roberto.'

He liked the way she said it. 'Her name was Marina, my nan.'

'That's kinda cute.'

'Her brothers were all cane cutters up in Queensland. But she came down here to Sydney when she got married and had my mum.'

She took long drags on her cigarette, closing her eyes as she blew out thin streams of smoke, which wafted upwards. He watched in silence.

'Is she a good cook?'

'Who?'

'Your nan. Spaghetti and meatballs and pizza and stuff?'

'She was a good cook,' he said, wishing he could stop remembering so much about Nan these days. Oh, lots and lots of things.

'Where is she, then?'

'Dead,' he said.

'And your mum?'

'Dead.'

'Wish mine was,' she laughed and sounded like Amanda for a minute. 'Real cow. And large as life, worse luck.' Flick, flick of the hair. 'Her last boyfriend nearly knocked my flaming teeth off my face. She didn't give a damn. Not her. She's out of it mostly.'

He didn't want to hear her life story—it was sure to be as bad as his.

But her voice changed and she peered at him again. 'So you're an orphan?'

He didn't want to say that his father was probably still alive somewhere. He didn't want to think about him at all. 'Yes.'

'You got a girlfriend?'

'No way,' he said, and felt himself blushing in the gloom.

'You like girls? Or boys?' and she laughed. 'Are you gay? You look it.'

'Girls,' he said.

'Sure?'

'Yeah.'

'Do you like Mandy?'

'Yeah.' He wished she'd stop questioning him like this.

'Lots and lots? Or a little bit? Or what?'

He was quiet.

'OK. OK. I can see you're a bleedin' babe in the wood.'

'I like Mandy lots and lots,' he said then.

She laughed. 'She's a bit of a crazy sometimes. When she's on it. Which is most of the time, these days.'

She put out her smoke and sniffed the air. 'Phew, you stink of fish or something.'

He blushed again. 'It's my jeans,' he said, showing her the smeared side of his leg.

'God, get some out of the bag over there. Mine'll fit you. It's OK—there's a bathroom along the hall. And water. Cold though.'

He rummaged through the bag. There were three or four pairs of jeans and any amount of T-shirts.

'Here, let me help.' She slid across the floor to the bag and held up a pair of jeans against him. 'They look all right. Have 'em. It's OK.'

He didn't want to change in front of this strange girl, so he took the jeans along to the bathroom. Funny that she noticed his smell when out here it was disgusting.

He should have a shower, he thought. It looked like it still worked. Only there was no soap and he felt too cold. He filled the rusty bath with water and dunked the dirty jeans but the slimy stain wouldn't lift.

'I left the jeans in the bath for a while,' he told her, back in the dark, stuffy room again.

'That's cool,' she said, 'maybe take 'em to the laundromat tomorrow. Someone'll pee on them—or worse—if you leave 'em there too long.'

He sat down again, trying to get used to the feel of the room. 'I got a tat today,' he told her.

'Gemma's work, I bet. If you show me yours, I'll show you mine.'

He pulled up his sleeve slowly and lifted the bandaid gently. He couldn't help grinning at the fat little frog he saw bouncing up his arm.

'Yuk! A frog. Just like Mandy's. Slimy little beasts.'

'I like it.'

'Sure. Sure. It's nice, I s'pose, if you go in for frogs and things. Real nice.'

She slid down on the floor, not attempting to show him her tats. 'Look, Robbie—Roberto—I'm just having a little rest for a while,' she told him. Within seconds she seemed fast asleep.

He wished she hadn't gone off to sleep and left him, but now he could take in the room without interruption. There was a window one end, covered with a tatty orange scarf and a fraying bamboo fan. A picture of the Virgin Mary hung above the broken wooden mantelpiece. He recognised it with a start. The large eyes of the pale-faced woman with the candle burning inside her chest and the pale blue scarf-thing over her head. A picture just like his nan had had so long ago at home. Hell, he had to stop thinking about her every five minutes! She was dead, gone, and Melanie might as well be too. Dead, gone, finished!

His gaze shifted round the room. There were candles in bottles here and there. The light mustn't work, he thought. Come to think of it there was no light up on the ceiling anyway. Just an empty socket at the end of a dangling cord. There seemed to be stuff everywhere, all over the floor. Maybe four or five separate piles. Cans, packets of syringes, packets of dead food too. And though it didn't smell like the hall, it was stale and airless.

A cockroach was making its way steadily down the fan at the window, its fat body moving clumsily. He watched it, fascinated. The biggest fella he'd seen yet. Well-fed for sure! It dropped to the floor and he heard it scuttle into one of the piles. He wondered how many cockroaches might be in a room like this, burrowing into the stuff all over, waiting for the dark. If you were still and you listened, you could hear the bloody things rustling round everywhere.

Four or five kids, he wondered, looking at the separate piles. And would they mind finding him here? With Tessa so heavily asleep and Amanda not here until late? Would they come in and be surprised to find him? Angry maybe? Tell him to go?

But as darkness fell and Tessa snored lightly beside him, cockroaches scampered through the dark and nobody came into the broken-down house. Nobody at all.

13

Violin

Robbie caught sight of a shock of white hair way up ahead. He wanted his money badly. He'd spent the last few notes Mandy had given him. He knew he'd have to face Pale and ask straight out for his share. Might as well be now.

'Pale. Heeey, Pale!' he called, running along the busy city street. People turned to stare at him, his voice was so loud and urgent.

But at the sound of his name the big boy darted on up the street and out of sight.

It wasn't fair. He'd done what Pale had asked and Pale had promised him a share. It wasn't bloody fair. He trudged on dejectedly. Pale was an out-and-out swine, tricking him like this. Pale was a——

'Gotcha!' A hand had him firmly by the collar, and then a laughing face was pushed into his. It was Pale, stepping out from a dark doorway and hooting with laughter.

'God, you're a gutless wonder. Should've seen the way you jumped then!'

Robbie wanted to ask straight off for the money. Maybe this ugly laughter of Pale's meant he was in a good mood. But Pale didn't stop talking.

'Guess what happened to me?' Pale was off up the street again so that Robbie had to run to keep up.

'Pity you weren't there. It was a real hoot, kid. Better than you in the sewer. See, I go down this back lane minding my own business and being a good boy. Then I come across a car. You can be lucky, you know. Didn't have to break in or anything. Some pigwit left the door unlocked! So I take a real good lookie. But this car doesn't have a cent and I get kind of angry. Not a bleedin' thing. Then just as I'm ready to get out, there's this case on the floor at the back. I hadn't seen it first time round, see. What's this, eh? A black case with a handle, real fancy. Maybe a million dollars inside?'

Pale had stopped again to laugh. 'Like hell! I pick up the box though. Kind of heavy. First off I think it's a guitar and I'll go and flog it. Or give it to Tessa 'cos she can play. Or some other jerk. But it's too small for a guitar. I open it up and I see it's a violin thing. A real old one, all shiny and polished up. All posh in this fancy case. So you know what I do?'

'No.' Robbie didn't want to know but there was no stopping the flood of Pale's story now.

'You'd've liked this, kid, would've cacked yourself.'

Robbie hated the way Pale laughed with that loud

hollow sound when he couldn't even crack a smile. He waited.

'I take the crummy violin thing out of its fancy black case, see. And do I do it over good! I belt it on this traffic sign first. Twang! a string breaks. My heart breaks. Ohhhh, dear me. I bash again. Twing, twang, the whole lot pops. Twing, twing, bloody twang. Jeez, I laughed. Then I belt that tricky box of music up and down that street. The wood's tougher than I think so I belt extra hard on the car, on the telegraph post, on the gutter. Thwack, wack! Should've seen it when I finished. Messy! Then I jumped on it. No more twing twang. What a shaaame. No more shine on it either. Then you know what I did?'

Robbie shook his head, not wanting to hear.

'This is the good bit. This is the bit where I cack myself and hope no pigs or anyone else's coming down the street. Careful as anything, see, I push every bit of that bloody broken thing back in its case. All the wood bits and bits of the twing twang and the soddin' knobs and bits of the handle. All of it. Just like a good boy I put that case right back where I found it in the car. And just like a good boy I lock the back of the car good.

'I nearly piss myself then thinking about somebody coming back to that car and driving wherever. And taking out that nice black box and opening it up to have a nice little play of their nice little fancy music thingo. And looking in and finding—Whaaaat! Sod all!'

Pale laughed so much Robbie thought it was a good

idea to join in.

'Can I have my money, Pale?' he asked when the big boy's laughter finally subsided. 'You said ... you said that ...'

'Sure thing, kid,' the big boy smiled as he spoke. 'When I'm good and ready.'

A fury mounted in Robbie, 'You said ...'

'You said, you said,' the big boy mimicked. 'Poor little dog face.' The Pale stopped smiling. 'Listen I need to talk to you. Not now ... Gotta go somewhere, meet someone—so not now. Something big, this is. I want you in on it, see. And so does my friend. You better meet me tomorrow, at the fountain, and I'll tell you. You can meet my friend, too. You'll like him. Lal. Big Lal. Yeah, you'll like him heaps. You be there, see, or I'll have to come and find you.'

Robbie nodded. Pale's face seemed so cruel and so close. Then he smiled again in that light-hearted way, making Robbie braver.

'The money, Pale. You said ...'

'Shut yer neck about the bleedin' money, you greasy creep.' And he was off down the street again, calling over his shoulder. 'Look down your pants, why doncha?'

Robbie found a wad of notes stuffed in his back pocket. Bleedin' idiot, he thought. Tears sprang to his eyes; not tears of relief, although he was glad of the feel of money. Tears of fury at the way Pale had managed to get at him even when he was *giving* him something.

He'd hated Pale's story about the violin. He'd felt like the violin himself, that's why. The smashed thing. He'd had to find laughter from some deep, frightened part of him that was wracked suddenly with a pain so bad he thought he might not be able to utter a sound. Laughter, when he'd wanted to cry out and cover his ears so he didn't have to hear any more.

Pale's story had reminded him of something else, of someone else. Of waking up in the night, long ago, to the sound of something being smashed in the room next door, of thumps and crashes—and of Melanie's hand that would sometimes reach out in the dark to take his.

14

Mandy

A long afternoon sitting, sitting in dappled sun by the fountain, waiting. He'd been in the pinball parlour but a kid there had pushed him round. He knew trouble when he saw it and so he'd left. He'd sauntered through the streets kicking a cigarette packet, until a cop had given him a look. Just a sideways glance. But he'd fled to the fountain to melt into the scene with the other kids that hung round there.

He'd seen Mandy again, on the other side of the road. But she seemed not quite the same Mandy.

'You can come with me if you like,' she'd said when he'd dodged across the road to greet her, all smiles. She seemed hurried and angry. He followed her though, down the street, round a corner, at top pace. A lane led them towards fire stairs that took them up two flights to a heavy metal door.

Mandy knocked and called. Several locks clicked and then a small dark girl flung open the door.

'Who's your boyfriend?' she asked.

'This is Robbie. He's OK.'

'Does Nathan know you're here?'

He saw Mandy's face change. Maybe Nathan was her boyfriend.

'Look I've got stuff for you. So are you letting us in or what? Show Robbie the joint, why don't you?'

'What's his other name?' the girl asked, eyeing him.

'What are ya?' Mandy blazed. 'A bleedin' cop now?'

'Armani,' said Robbie, burying his father's name forever and finding comfort in his nan's.

The girl laughed. 'Jerks' suits, eh?' but Robbie didn't know what she meant.

'Suits rich guys wear, der. Armani suits!'

'Oh.' He didn't know whether he liked Mandy's friend.

They went into a large dim room, more like a hall, with a dance floor way down the other end. It seemed almost empty but Robbie could make out paintings on the walls, all the way round.

'There's a full-on bar over here,' she told Robbie proudly, 'and down there we're setting up for the dance show tonight. I'll put the lights on. Mandy's dancing if she's not too smashed.'

She poured them both a drink from a giant Coke bottle and he took it eagerly. It was hot and dusty in here and he didn't like it.

'I like dancing,' Mandy told him. Already she sounded different, had moved away from him.

They stayed a long time—too long, he thought later—in the dark hall with the full-on bar and the lighted squares of dance floor. Mandy and the dark-haired girl, who never told him her name, got into some stuff he knew. He saw the flash of syringes as they went out of the big room. And they seemed different when they came back, or at least Mandy did.

The other girl put on music and set some disco lights going. He didn't like the look of Mandy now at all. He leaned against the wall and watched.

She danced in an ugly way, with big awkward, lunging movements, her legs flying up and out, her pumping arms, thin and jerky. Her face had a fake smile, too, and he felt like crying. Under the grotesquerie of lights—now yellow now red now green—her face seemed a blotch of dark holes. Eye holes, nose holes and a big gaping mouth hole. And the music was extra ugly too—like nothing he'd heard before—city noises and rock and then other indescribable sounds, so loud the place shook. He felt he couldn't bear it, put his hands over his ears and closed his eyes, but hands grasped at him.

The other girl had grabbed him. She led him onto the dance floor with its on–off chequerboard of blueish, whitish, glary lights

'Dance, you,' and she'd gyrated her hips against his. He ran from the noise, the lights and the girl's laughter and threw himself down behind the bar.

Mandy found him there. 'What's wrong with you?'

Her face was streaked with sweat and colour had run down from her eyelashes. She seemed cold, hot, different.

'Nothing.'

She knelt down beside him and he smelled the sourness of her breath. 'Kiss me,' she demanded. Her face was close to his, 'You want to, don't you? Go on. Kiss me.'

'Get away,' he called in panic, as the face, the one full of holes, came close to his again.

'Get off' he yelled, sounding like Pale. 'You slut!'

He didn't know why he said that; he didn't mean it. Mandy was his friend, his only friend here. What made him say that to her? Maybe that Coke she'd given him had something in it.

He saw her face change. 'Dead right there,' she said, getting up. She walked across the floor and out the door to hoots of laughter from the other girl who was dancing alone on the flashing floor.

Robbie sat for a moment not knowing what to do, whether to call out, but the music was too loud. He jumped up and ran after her, but when he was out in the dazzling daylight of the fire stair landing Mandy was gone. And so, he soon discovered, was most of the money in his back pocket.

15

Getting Closer

Robbie made his way through the long grass, moving towards the duckpond. He saw the old lady quite clearly. She was walking slowly and once or twice he was sure she glanced his way. Would she scream blue murder? There were plenty of people about. 'There, that's him. That's the boy who ...'

When the stepped out into the bright morning light he knew she saw him but her expression didn't change. She sat down on the bench and stared out at the water. The ducks, all-knowing, even the far-away ducks straggling round the island, began their journey towards her. He did, too.

He came close to the seat, over the soft, clipped grass, quietly. At a clump of banana plants he stopped. Again he felt she could see him from the corner of her eye, but she didn't turn her head.

Past the seat, near the water, he sat himself down on the ground, staring ahead as the ducks approached.

Clouds banked up over the pampas grass on the island and the ducks, bored with waiting for bread, began drifting away. He sat on, not sure why. Some light, strong thread-thing seemed to extend from him to the old lady. Maybe he wanted to say something to her. Or maybe he wanted her to say something to him. Then he heard her sigh and imagined she was climbing to her feet. Yes, she was walking away. He could hear her footsteps.

On his way back across the park he thought he should have talked to her. Well, next time he would, they would. There'd be no trick, no cops, no Home. He was sure of that much. He'd talk to her next time. Thinking about this made things look brighter, a whole heap brighter. As if he'd run into Mandy again and it would be all right. As if tomorrow was going to be a good day.

'Some days are golden,' his nan used to say, 'just golden. Not many, mind, but there are some. Mornings were silver in my city with all that water. Silver mornings on the water. And golden days,' she told him. 'Days for singing things and praying and then feasting and being happy.'

She'd say these things quietly because his father would get good and mad if he heard Nan talking of happy days. He'd get furious if ever she so much as mentioned the word Italy, let alone show him the pictures she kept hidden.

'You bleedin' immigrants—all the same. Well, what are you doing here if it's that bleedin' marvellous back

there?' he'd ask, his voice thick with insult and anger.
'What in the hell are you doing here? Tell me that. Go
on. Tell me all about it!'

And he knew she'd be forced to tell her story again.
How her father and brothers had cane-cutting jobs in
Queensland. And how grateful they were, she was. That
Australia had been so good to them. Better than Italy
could ever be ...

He hated hearing his grandmother yelled at like that.
The way one word from his father could make her so
meek. The way she was so afraid of the loud voice and
big angry fists that could beat the table, or anyone in
their path.

When his grandmother had gone to the hospital he
had everything to fear from his father. For Nan had
shielded them as best she could. And Nan could talk
him out of rages sometimes. But with Nan gone, he and
Melanie had kept right out of his dad's way. Maybe his
mum dying was what had made his father so mean. But
no, not really. He'd been cruel to her too, Nan said.
There was cruelty in his heart, Nan said. Must have
been, or else he couldn't have treated his kids the way
he did. Drink or no drink, he was a bully. Even when his
mother was alive, his father had been a bully. And
bullies like him can only get worse, his nan had said.

'You and Melanie—you've got to get away from
him,' Nan said on that terrible night. 'We're not going
to be afraid of him ever again.' She dabbed at his cut lip
and then at the tears in her own eyes. 'I'm going to find

us somewhere, that's why. The lady in the new fruit shop, she told me about Elsie's. It's a place we can all go for a while. Where he can't come. Now listen to me good, Robbie. When he goes down to the pub tonight I'm going to grab our things together. I'm going to wake you and Mel and we're going. And it's going to be OK.'

But when he'd woken up, it was morning and he could hear his father's heavy, angry movements in the kitchen. And not Nan's light quick movements. And when he got up, anxious, calling for her, his dad had told him.

'She's sick. Gone to the hospital. Too sick for you kids to see. And don't you go whining about it neither.'

He could see Nan's packed bag standing in the hallway but he didn't dare to ask about it.

The lady in the park looked nothing like his dark-haired grandmother, yet he was reminded of her so much. He thought her voice would be quiet, and the smell of her would be like flowers—like Nan. Next time he'd speak to her. They'd speak and he'd tell her he was sorry, he was resolved.

So Robbie had come back again the next day. There was a gang he'd run into three times already round the Cross. He needed to ask Pale about those kids. He was dead scared of them, specially one of the boys. The park felt safer, and he might run into her.

When the park toilets were opened later in the morning he washed as well as he could in the basin, drying his face and his hands on a long piece of scrappy paper towel. The face in the murky mirror almost frightened him.

The bins offered up scraps of meat at lunchtime. There'd been a big barbeque over by the bike track. He found meat all wrapped neatly in tomato-sauce-smeared paper napkins. And he could hardly believe it—whole slices of banana cake, untouched. He couldn't go hungry today. He was glad, for food in his stomach made him feel safer. Food in his stomach meant he could think things out better and say things properly, too.

He was aware of the hours ticking over, but something, someone was making him stay here. The mothers and their babies came and went. He liked watching the babies, the way they laughed so easy and cried so easy, too, come to think of it. And the way they staggered around everywhere, the little ones, as if the whole world, this part of it anyway, belonged to them.

The diners at the jerks' restaurant across the road came and went. The cyclists and the joggers, all decked out in their fancy gear, came and went. And as the afternoon wore on, the walkers turned out. Older men and women going briskly and some real oldies strolling along, holding hands. Waiting, waiting. Where was she, the grandmother person right now? And would she come back to her seat by the pond like he figured?

He climbed to his feet at the first sight of that soft wavy hair in the sunlight. Yeay, she was coming! But then in a flash he saw that she was not alone. There was a boy running up behind her and then walking beside her. A boy younger than him, holding her hand and yapping like mad to her. Robbie slipped back into the shadow of the banana plants.

He saw how carefully she listened to the boy and felt a terrible pang, a dark, angry feeling of useless jealousy. They passed by, went to the water's edge and threw blobs of bread to the noisy, jostling ducks.

Then she walked back to her seat and, instead of sitting down, reached under the cement base and stashed something there, just out of sight. Hidden among the fat leaves, he had a moment of real happiness. She was stashing something for him, so she'd been thinking of *him*!

Somehow the young boy's voice didn't seem quite so annoying as they passed by him again. Later he knelt by the seat and reached under. There were sandwiches, a whole stack of them, and some fruit in a plastic bag. Dinner!

16

Lal

Pale was excited. 'You can get in that place easy, Robbie. Lal told me about it. I've been past the joint more times than I'd like to say. There's a window— small, with broken bars. Has to be a little kid gets in. That's why we thought of you, see. I told Lal how cool you were at Bondi too. I swear it's easy as taking candy.'

Robbie had heard these words before.

'You can get through and let me in. Nothing more. Don't even have to stay around. I'll lift the stuff. Fix you up later. I gave you something from the ghetto blaster, now didn't I? So how about it?'

'Nah.'

Pale caught him by the arm. 'Lal might get real angry if you say no.' Lal the rock spider.

'No. I don't want ...'

'Look, I'm your friend, aren't I?'

'You said you shouldn't have friends,' Robbie said

obstinately.

'Streeties have all got to be friends,' Pale said, all quiet and sugary.

'Listen kid,' Pale's voice took another tone, more urgent. 'I'm doing this for me, for sure. I never pretend. But you know how you've been looking for Mandy. Well, Mandy's real sick. That's why she's not back at the squat. I know where she is but she wants to be alone. She needs some stuff very bad and she can't work at the moment she's that sick. Her boyfriend knocked her around and pissed off again.

'So you're doing it for Mandy?'

'Kind of. Well, some of its for her.'

Their eyes met a moment. 'Enough,' Pale said.

Robbie had asked Pale about Mandy. He'd been back to the squat and she hadn't been there. Nor had the girl called Tessa. The noisy group of boys and girls didn't know where she was either.

'Her stuff's gone,' a thin red-headed girl with exaggerated black around her eyes loomed at him out of the dark. 'But that don't mean a thing. She often takes it and goes off a while. And then she brings it back.'

'They put her in detox, I bet,' another voice.

'Nah—she's probably pissed off in a white Mercedes to get married,' someone else called out. 'I saw one out front.'

'Shut up, Trent. Relax, kid,' the red-haired girl went on. 'Come on in.'

But the loud noise of a ghetto blaster grated on his

nerves and he didn't want to stay there without Mandy.

'Look,' the red-haired girl said, following him down the hall. 'Round this place, people come and people go. It's no big deal. You gotta get used to it. A girl like Mandy—she can look after herself. She'll be fine.'

He wondered if it were true about Mandy being sick. About Pale wanting to help her. It was hard to think of Pale helping anyone.

'All you gotta do is crawl in the window. It's an easy fall to the floor and I can see a side door with a bar across it. Don't seem to be no alarms either. My friend Lal's checked it out and he knows about these things. You open the side door and then you can shoot through. Easy as that. I've checked it out from the front as well. Real old fella there at night, at closing time. Easy as taking candy from a baby.'

Why did Pale always say that?

'But you won't ... you won't ...?' Robbie was frightened to ask, remembering Pale's stories about his knife.

'Won't what?'

'Do anything to him.'

'What do you think?' Pale glanced at Robbie's anxious face. 'No way. The old bloke'll be scared witless anyway. No worries. Now come on and meet my friend Lal.'

Robbie didn't like Lal from the first. Something about the way he half smiled and didn't look at you all the time he was talking. Like he was having a joke on you. Something about the way he spoke to Pale, too, kind of bossy and as if Pale was a real fool. Of course he was a lot older than Pale and a whole lot more powerful. At times, though, he spoke as if Robbie wasn't there at all.

'He won't chicken out will he?' Lal asked when Pale had told him the plan about dropping Robbie through the window to open the side door for them.

'No way,' Pale had said so heartily that Robbie recognised Pale's fear for the first time. 'Will you, kid?'

'He won't blabber neither?'

'Not this kid,' Pale assured him.

How could be Pale be so sure? The way he spoke like that. Pale'd only known him a few days.

'I've got something for kids who blab,' Lal said, now looking at Pale but drawing out a flick knife even meaner looking than Pale's. It glinted in the half light.

'My friend here,' and he smiled, caressing the blade, still not looking at Robbie. Never looking at Robbie. 'My little friend does real nice work, too. If he's asked, that is. Pale knows.'

'Put a lid on it, Lal. I've told you, the kid's OK.'

'But just in case,' Lal said in that lazy smiling way, 'just in case, I thought he should know all about my friend. My friend doesn't like snotty-nosed nerds of kids who talk too much.'

'Has Lal ever totalled anyone?' Robbie asked as they made their way somewhere Pale had said was good for the night.

'Nah. He's all talk, kid. All talk.'

But Robbie wasn't so sure.

On the way Pale stopped at a shop and bought chocolate and a small carton of milk. He paid, too. 'We'll have a cuppa tea,' he joked.

The streets seemed narrower and meaner here, and the lanes more twisted.

'This place is neat for tripping. Real neat,' Pale said, turning down a pathway. 'But don't blab on about it to nobody. Only Lal and me know it. Good hideout, see.'

17

Cats

Robbie saw a great, yawning, dark hole stopped up with a few straggly strands of barbed wire. It was a viaduct nestled in against a looming cliff face.

'Looks worse than it is,' Pale said when Robbie stopped in his tracks. 'Honest. It's dry,' he insisted, 'and real warm inside.'

They went in. At first there was the almost comforting smell of an underground railway station. But deeper inside the stench of cat and human urine filled his nostrils. His feet stumbled over cans and God knows what other rubbish strewn across an earthen floor. Cockroaches and something bigger seemed to scuttle off as they groped their way inside. He thought he might turn back to the light, get right out of there, but Pale had grabbed his arm.

'You'll get used to it in no time.'

Then Pale's voice changed so completely that Robbie could scarcely believe his ears. 'Puss, here puss,' Pale sang softly through the darkness. 'Puss, here puss,' as if he were at the backdoor of a regular house, about to feed a regular cat! 'We're here, pussycat!'

Robbie could almost have laughed but he jumped as he felt the body of a cat brushing against his leg and heard its purr.

'So where you put him, eh?' The same soft unfamiliar tone from Pale. 'Where?'

'There were four of them,' he told Robbie. 'They carked it, the others. But one of them's a tough little blighter, like me. He made it. The white one! All white. I feed it now. And the mum.'

Robbie stood amazed. Pale, who'd said you shouldn't like anyone or anything, coming into this stinking cesspool to feed a kitten and a mother cat!

Pale led him deeper inside, turning a corner so that Robbie was sure he'd never find his way out to the light again by himself. He hoped Pale wouldn't let go of his T-shirt, leaving him alone here.

'See what I got here. A torch for one thing,' Pale was proud to show him and flicked it on. 'From the hardware shop. Beauty! Cost a packet if you paid. And lookie here!'

He was just like a kid, Robbie thought, showing off toys and treasure.

In the strong torchlight Robbie could see a deep brick recess with a packed-earth floor. It was tidily stacked. Like a bedroom really. A plank with two bricks and some tins and bottles in a row. A kind of bed—well, a pillow on a sleeping bag. A ghetto blaster next to that, smaller than the one they'd nicked at the beach, a bulging backpack, and some bricks, lined up neatly.

'Just in case, you know ...' Pale fingered a brick and with a shiver Robbie heard echoes of Lal's voice. 'My friend. If some yobs come in, looking for a bit of action. A brick in the right direction——' he laughed.

'Now come on, catface.' He opened the milk carton and picked up a greasy lid that had acted as a saucer before tonight. The mother cat lapped at the milk hungrily. 'Leave some, prat,' he said, but he refilled the lid and scratched her gently behind the ears.

'Show me where you put the kitty cat. She moves it round, see. Real smart,' and he left, following the mother cat as she went surely into the dark. Robbie sank down on the bed. He wouldn't stay the night here. When Pale fell asleep he'd be off. He'd never get used to the stink of the place, or the blackness of it either.

The quiet was suddenly shattered. A terrible cry from the direction Pale had gone brought Robbie to his feet. He'd been bleedin' murdered down there. Murdered for sure!

Then he heard a voice again. NO—Pale was alive, well and truly. His voice was loud and thick with hatred and anger. 'Soddin' jerk, soddin' soddin' jerk.'

There was a furious stamping sound, tins crashing against the wall, breaking glass and then deep breathing and another sound. Like a little kid whimpering.

Robbie dared not move. He waited and the seconds

ticked by heavily in that dark place. When Pale came
staggering back, he threw himself on the ground,
shaking with sobs of rage. A torrent of abuse and anger
poured from his lips, then incomprehensible words.
There seemed to be foam around his lips. He'd gone off
his rocker for sure. He seemed in some kind of terrible
agony as he writhed and rocked and swore and cried.
Was it drugs making him go crazy or what?

The torch had fallen to the floor where it lit up the
brick wall and Pale, his fists beating the dusty ground in
waves of rage. Robbie pushed his back against the wall,
trying to take up as little room as possible, waiting for
this unaccountable storm to pass.

Gradually, Pale's sobs and curses ceased. He rolled
over, sat up and rubbed his nose and eyes with his
sleeve.

'Pale? You OK?'

'OK,' the big boy spoke at last but it sounded like a
recorded message. 'It's OK. Sure, it's OK. It's OK.'

'What hap ...'

'That dogbreath, Lal. Has to be.'

Pale opened a stubby with his teeth and took a good
long draught. He was quiet for several minutes and in
the silence Robbie read his change of mood.

'Lal's work down there,' Pale's ordinary voice said.
'Take the torch. Go take a look. You gotta grow up one
day. Go take a soddin' look!'

Robbie knew he had to do as he was told.

'You can't miss it.'

The torch beam was eerie on the walls of that place. He thought it'd reveal rats, at the very least—and after that, what? What terrible thing had made Pale blubber like a kid and rage like a maniac. What? Maybe he already knew. Maybe he could pretend he'd looked. But maybe he needed to know once and for all. 'To grow up fast', like Pale had said.

But when he saw it he felt as if he would throw up. He dropped the torch and gagged but his stomach was empty. Behind him Pale's hollow laughter was ringing right through that empty space. 'Bleedin' pretty sight?'

Robbie's knees were shaking and it took a long time to make his way back to where Pale sat, propped against the wall, drinking.

Later that night, though, it was as if nothing had happened. It was as if that sight at the end of the tunnel didn't exist. Pale was almost businesslike about tomorrow, and friendly. Was Pale mad or was he?

'Gotta meet Lal tomorrow, six sharp. Right here. Outside.'

How could he talk in that normal voice about Lal?

'So you be here, won't you? Gotta do the job for Lal. OK?'

'Sure.'

They lay back on their makeshift beds.

'Here, have some.' Pale held out a tinny.

He took another swig. It was making his head feel fuzzy and nice, making him feel like agreeing with Pale

and forgetting everything else. Almost happy, floating
in the dark with a friend beside him.

'Pale?'

'Yeah?'

'You ever been on a river?'

'Been up the river,' the big boy laughed. 'Too many
times.'

'No, I mean in a boat.'

'Been over the harbour on one of those hovercraft
things. In a storm. Cool, but there were school kids on
board. Nerds of school kids. Lots of them spewing,
too—it was that rough.'

'You go to school?'

'Course I did,' he sounded angry. 'Everyone goes to
school.'

'Did you like school?'

'Me? No way. No one likes school. School's for
dimwits. Dimwits, ders and deadbeats!'

'Sometimes I think about school, you know.'

'Yeah?'

'Like, I'd like to go back and learn and get smart.'

'You can get smart around here,' Pale laughed, 'You
can get real smart.'

'Like, I'd like to read some books.'

Pale snorted. 'Jesus. Read some books. What are ya?'

'Wouldn't you like to?'

'Nah, I wouldn't like to.' He sucked noisily from the
can. 'Books are no bleedin' good to me. Just like school
was no bleedin' good for me. They didn't even teach me

to read. No way. So much for their bleedin' schools.'

'You mean you can't read?'

'Shut your face, kid. I'm kinda tired.' He chucked the tin can so hard against a pillar it bounded halfway across the space to the opening. And then he made a loud belching noise and fell silent. When the mother cat came nosing round them he pushed her away.

Robbie stared up into the dark. He'd concentrate on the silver river. Imagine sunlight and he wouldn't think about the end of the tunnel. But there were noises, the sound of shuffling, uncertain footsteps.

'What's that?' Robbie whispered.

'Sometimes whopper rats round here. Just chuck something at 'em.'

'No, there it is again.'

Pale got up and disappeared for a minute. 'It's cool,' he said, reappearing. 'This old fella he comes in. When the old men's place is filled up. He's OK. Him and his White Lady.'

An old man in thick layers of clothing came towards them. Robbie knew there were bag ladies all round the Cross. He looked around for the old man's companion, but he shuffled past them to his own corner alone. In a few minutes, there was a strong smell of methylated spirits.

Pale seemed in a talkative mood again. Robbie made little grunts every now and again to show he was listening, until he heard Mandy's name.

'You better quit looking for her—Mandy. She's got

this boyfriend. And a big habit. They kind of go together. And he likes to keep her working when she's well enough.'

'Working?'

'Hell, kid, you know what Mandy does. She's on the game, you der—or are you more stupid than I thought? Flogs her body.'

'Sure, I knew it,' he said, but he felt cold inside, thinking of Mandy and of Mandy's boyfriend.

'Nathan doesn't like her getting too friendly with anyone, neither. So you better not go looking anymore. I mean, I can get to her without anybody knowing,' he boasted, 'but you—you better give up trying. Want some?' he was getting a syringe out of his bag.

'Nah.' Robbie lay there, staring at the dark. He wished he hadn't said anything about Mandy. It seemed like Pale wanted to smash into everything that was his, just like he'd smashed the violin. Just like his own life was kind of smashed up already. Pale, thank God, was asleep now, snoring badly. Robbie closed his eyes.

No matter what he told himself, no matter what he tried to picture in his mind, words, people, places faded. Even Mandy. Even the old lady. And he saw the small furry body of the kitten, its eyes and its baby pink tongue popping out. Its white furry neck stretched long. A spray of dried blood splashed down its fat little body. It had been strangled by a piece of fine wire, extending from pillar to pillar, which had been looped tightly around its neck.

18

Iris Walker

The park again. It was a pleasing bright green under the storm clouds. He'd longed for the streets of the Cross all the time he'd been in the foster home and then briefly in that other place. Longed for the friends he'd been told about. But lots of times he found his way here to the park. To hide alone, away from the streets. He didn't like Pale's places, and Mandy—maybe he'd never find her now, trace her anywhere. The wide open spaces of the park soothed him a little, and when he felt bad something always drew him towards the pond. Looking for her, the old lady, he supposed, but he hadn't seen her again.

Yet, and his heart skipped a beat, he was sure he could see her right now. On the seat by the banana plants, and by herself. She looked up. She could still yell the place down, bring people running, but when he got close enough she said loud and firm, 'I've been waiting for you. I'm glad you got here.'

He sat uneasily at the end of her bench, feeling shy and stupid, finding not a word to say to her. Still, he didn't move away, and as he'd hoped, she began to talk to him.

She didn't ask him a whole string of questions. She didn't ask him about his mum or his home. She didn't comment, as he thought she might, that he was an immigrant and ask which country he was from. She just asked if he was OK or if he was hungry. She told him she knew boys just like him. And then she went on as if she'd known him for ages.

'Your hands look just like my son's. When he was your age,' she remarked.

Something about the way she said it made him ask, 'Is he dead?'

'Mark. Yes, he is. He died unexpectedly when he was young. Well, he was sixteen. A car accident on the Pacific Highway. My old house was not far from the Pacific Highway. A mate was driving him home from a sports afternoon. Quite a while ago now.' She stared out at the duckpond a while. 'But you never get over the death of a child,' she told him.

He thought that you probably couldn't if you were a mother like her. Or like his nan.

He liked the way she was telling him things about herself and not asking and asking questions. It was good sitting here listening. All about her house, and every room.

'That's why I found it hard to leave my home, up

north, and come to live here in the city,' she went on. 'Mark loved the place as much as I did. As much as I do.'

'Well, why'd you go and leave it?' he asked.

'Oh things change, you know. You get older and tireder.'

He thought she didn't look old and tired at all.

'And my daughter lives in one of those big old houses beside the park. She has a flat up the back for me. It's nice. Very nice. But I miss the river. I dream about it, you know.'

His heart gave a little thump when she said that.

'The river?'

'Yes. Rochedale—that's the name of my place—is right on the bend in the river. The road's called just that—The Bend—by the locals. Right on the big Clarence River. I've lived up around that river all my life. If it weren't for this park, you know, and the birds and the ducks and the ponds, I'd go crazy.' She took his arm. 'Look! Do you see that rainbow over there? Just behind the island?'

He nodded, for he could see the faint pencilling of it against the dark sky.

'That's why I like coming here,' she told him. 'You can see things like that. Nature. It's a good sign, a rainbow, don't you think? And you know my name–Iris – that means rainbow!'

'I got a tat,' he offered his arm. The bandaid was gone now, and the scab as well. Just the bright tattoo, leaping so happily up his arm. He wondered if she'd think it nasty.

'Oh, a tattoo,' and she looked closely, holding his hand in her own warm one. 'A very nice one, too. I like frogs. Back home they're all over the pond in my front yard. Funny how you don't seem to get them in cities any more. Frogs are good luck, you know.'

'I better go,' he said.

She put her hand out towards him again, but this time to shake his. 'Well, my name's Iris Walker. If you should need me, I live in that house, the grey one over there. At the back of it, that is, in a flat. If ever——'

'And I'm Robbie,' he said.

She shook his hand warmly.

'I've got to go,' he said.

'Will you come back soon?'

'I don't know,' he answered truthfully. 'See, I've got to find this friend, Mandy and ...'

'Well, I hope you find her. And I hope I see you again.' She smiled, but now she looked a bit sad.

Robbie smiled back at her. Mandy was his true friend all right, and he had to find her again, but he was glad he'd talked to the old lady, at last. Without saying it he had let her know he was sorry for what had happened.

But she was from another world, he knew that. With her big grey house near the park, with her letterboxes and front-door key and grandson. Another world that wasn't his, couldn't be his. He was glad he'd talked to her, though. Funny how she was just like his nan, he thought, wanting and wanting the river.

'You should go home,' he told her.

'Oh, I'm strolling back after I've fed the ducks. It's probably going to rain.'

'No, I mean home. To the river,' he said.

She gave him such a funny look when he said that, and then she sighed. 'Harder than you think,' she murmured.

'You should go anyway.'

'I'm glad you've found a friend,' she said, abruptly changing the subject. 'That's one of the most important things in the world, a friend,' but again she sounded sad.

He wouldn't meet Pale and Lal at six sharp. No, he wouldn't. He'd find the guts to go into the City Mission place and see if Mandy was there, or if they knew ... He had to get going.

'See ya,' he said, turning to go.

'Bye, Robbie,' she called after. 'Remember what I said—if you need help.' But she thought that she would probably never see him again.

19
TV

He pushed open the door. In the front room there were two huddled figures on lounges, both of them fast asleep. In the larger sitting room beyond it there were six or seven kids, all watching television, and a young woman.

'Come on in,' she said with a smile, coming to the door. 'I've seen you standing at the window lots of times. What's your name?'

'Mark,' he told her.

'Well come in, Mark. There's some coffee and biscuits on the table. Help yourself.'

'I'm looking for someone.'

'Yeah?'

Not one of the kids had looked up from the TV.

'Mandy. My sister. Kind of tall with dark curly hair and ...'

'Mandy who?'

'It doesn't matter,' he said, turning. 'I thought she

might have come in here. She told me to come here. It's OK, I'm going.'

'You got a place?' the young woman asked, following him into the outer room again, ''cause if you haven't ...'

'It's OK,' he said, 'I've got a place.'

'Well, if someone called Mandy comes in and fits your description, I'll tell her that her brother Mark was looking for her, right?'

'Thanks,' he said and was out onto the street again.

The wind was blowing and a piece of newspaper flapped against his leg. He kicked it off and it soared away down the grimy street. Useless jerk. Useless jerk. He said the words over and over in his head as he trudged the street, eyes down. That's what I am. When he looked up there was that gang, just across the street, and that boy, the one who'd yelled ugly things at him, who was itching to push him around.

'Changed your mind?' the young woman at the mission place asked as she opened the door.

'Yeah.' He was panting.

She glanced across the road and saw the big boy lounging against the wall of the fire station.

'Look, I know him. If he's bothering you, I can call the police.'

'No.' His voice was sharp. 'I mean—no, it's OK.'

'Well, come on in and watch some TV.'

He sat on the shabby lounge and watched a show about people who lived in neat homes in a neat street.

Homes that had front fences and neat squares of lawn.
A blond, smiling girl was walking up the path and on
her arm there was a blond, smiling boy.

He'd have to connect with Pale and Lal again. Have
to. Because he didn't know what to do about the kid out
in the street there, or the gang. If he was going to stay
here he needed people like Pale and Lal. He'd have to
meet them and he'd have to do the job. And go on doing
their lousy jobs. The TV music was rising as the blond
pair held hands and walked towards their neat front
door. Bleedin' TV.

He'd never get away from them, from people like
Pale and Lal, never. He blinked away tears of
realisation. He was trapped again, and it had only taken
a few days to get into a current so deep he couldn't get
out.

He'd meet them tonight, of course. He'd go early, as
if going early would make the whole thing over with
sooner. And he'd take some of Pale's dope or get some.
Might as well.

20

A Pushover

Halfway down the lane, Lal's lazy, smiling tone had changed. He'd ignored Robbie when he'd turned up at six sharp, and continued to ignore him as they walked through the darkening streets. But he'd talked non-stop to Pale. How could Pale give the time of day to this sneering jerk after he'd done that disgusting thing. But Robbie recognised Pale's whining tone. Scared–friendly. Dead-scared like he'd been himself in the Home place, and kind of pleading. Only there the Home people had hated him for it. Lal seemed to like Pale being like this. Like a dog trotting after him. He felt sick listening to them.

Halfway down the lane, Lal's manner had changed. He'd grabbed Pale by the scruff of the neck and pushed him against the wall as if he were about to thump him.

'Hey!' Pale was winded, surprised, his eyes wide with fear.

'You're not going to run off anywhere? After this little job, like?' Lal demanded.

'No way.'

'And no handouts to friends or rellies?'

'Are you kidding?'

'You owe me, remember. You owe me heaps.'

'I know, Lal.'

'Good. Just so's we understand one another.' Lal relaxed his grip. 'You've explained all that to the kid?'

'He'll be fine. He'll do what he's told. Just fine.'

'Good.'

Lal walked on and Pale fell in beside him again as if nothing had happened. 'It's all under control, mate,' Pale assured him.

Robbie noticed that Pale's whole manner seemed to change suddenly, become more confident, as something changed hands. And Robbie could see, despite the darkness and the swiftness of that exchange, just what it was.

'No need to use it,' Lal told him.

'No need to use it.'

Why was Pale repeating it like a parrot, Robbie wondered.

'It's in case, see. Just a nice little tap on the head if there's any trouble. He's an old guy. Counts the takings last thing every night. I've watched from the front. A pushover, I reckon.'

Robbie hadn't expected this. He'd thought—Pale had said—he'd just have to open the back door, the one from the lane, and then Pale'd take the stuff and they'd go. Pale had said that he wouldn't hurt the old guy—and now he'd slipped that thing into his coat pocket. He'd been scared of Lal, of course, with his knife and his funny talk. But now he was more scared of Pale with 'a friend' in his pocket. He could run off, but Pale already had him by the arm as if he had guessed what Robbie was thinking. And they went on threading their way though the bins and plastic bags, down yet another narrow back lane. It was dark, gritty and cold and the wind kept lunging things at them, but Pale didn't seem to notice.

'This is it,' Pale said, sounding pleased. Lal seemed to have evaporated. It was at street level, right at their feet, a tiny window with bent bars and a smashed frame.

Robbie stood in the gutter and peered down. 'Jesus! I can't fit through there.'

'Kneel down,' Pale commanded in the hard voice he'd used in the sewer outlet. 'Go on. Do like I say. Kneel!'

Robbie felt the heavy pressure of Pale's hand on his shoulder and knelt.

'Take a good lookie. It's bigger than you think, now isn't it?'

'Well, don't kick me then,' said Robbie, glancing up at Pale's face.

'I'd never do that.' Pale's voice sounded just like Lal's now. 'Come on. Don't hang about. Pigs come round here all the time.'

And then, as Robbie hesitated at the small opening, he felt a cold hand on the back of his neck.

It was Pale's own voice again, 'Shove your head through there now, dogbreath, or I'll do it for you!'

There was no getting away from him either. 'OK, OK.' Robbie said, 'Only get offa me.'

He spat on his hands so they would grip the inside wall better. Kneeling down, peering into a dimly lit hallway, he thought the window frame did seem bigger than he'd first thought. But not that much bigger.

'All you gotta do,' Pale was coaxing now, 'is get through there. A bit of a squeeze, but you'll make it no trouble. Jump down and open the door. I won't touch you. Promise.'

Halfway in, Robbie thought his ribs might crack. But then suddenly, surprisingly, the bulk of him was through the broken frame and he could breathe again. He steadied himself with his hands on the wall. Then he was on the floor and inside. He looked around. It seemed such a long way down that hallway, past another closed door, the one that led into the shop. A radio was playing in there. He stopped, frozen for a moment. But then he saw a large bolt quite clearly and moved towards it.

'Go on. Open it,' he heard Pale's urgent whisper. As if he didn't know what to do.

Four, five, six steps—he was at the door. The bolt was heavy, but it should have slid back easily enough. He was fumbling because of the sweat on his hands. He was shivering with cold and yet his hands were sweating, all the more because he knew Pale was on the other side of the door with that something in his pocket. That something he feared more than the idea of being caught. God! he couldn't budge it, and Pale'd be getting more and more ...

He wiped his hands down his jeans. He could hear his own breathing, so loud he was sure they could hear it inside the shop. Right through the closed door, louder than the music. He heaved the bolt again and this time his grip held and the thing slid back. With a twist of the heavy brass handle, the door to the laneway stood wide open. And there was Pale, cool as a cucumber, grinning at him on the step.

Maybe he could just duck straight out into the safety of the dark and leave Pale to it. But Pale advanced on him, still smiling, and took his arm again. 'Open the door.'

'I just have!'

'The other door, dimwit!'

There was no disobeying him. Pale had one hand in his pocket. With the other he dragged Robbie through the second door, the one Robbie had pushed open so timidly, so quietly. And there they were in the blueish light of the closed shop. There was the old man, just as Lal had said. He had his back to them and his head down, mumbling to himself at the open cash register. The radio was playing louder in here and the old man was humming the tune. Robbie could hear the words clearly. *You made me love you. I didn't want to do it. I didn't want to do it.* He was so close to the old man he could easily have reached out and touched him.

21

Madness

'What do you mean you saw the boy? The boy who attacked you?'

'As I say—the younger one.'

'You saw him in broad daylight? The one that ...'

'The boy. Yes.'

'And you say you spoke to him?'

'Yes. And it was as I thought. Hungry for love, that child.'

'Mum, I don't understand what it is you're trying to do. Why didn't you go to the police at once?'

Iris understood her daughter's anger, she'd expected it. But she felt duty-bound to tell her what had happened at the park. Now she saw all the unpleasantly familiar signs: her daughter's darkening eyes, the red blotches rising on her neck, the slightly raised voice, the look of incredulity. But she was undaunted. The talk with Robbie had been worth her daughter's anger. Anyway, wasn't Jane always angry these days? Every little thing seemed to cause a flare up, Ben's slightest misdemeanour. And she was sure it was because she was living here. She, Iris Walker, was no longer a friend to her daughter, but a duty, a burden.

Today in the park she'd felt as if she'd talked to a friend, young as he was. And just like the old times she'd sensed that the boy was all right. Not like the older boy he'd been with, who'd been left running wild too long now. Not like that. The young boy could still hear her.

'I don't expect you to understand, Jane. But I had to tell you because I invited him here. That is if he felt he could cope with ...'

'If he could cope! Mum, this is madness!' Jane exploded. 'Inviting a street kid to our house. To my house. Endangering us in this way! What's got into you, Mum?'

'An opportunity,' Iris said calmly.

Jane laughed, a dry, unhumorous sound. 'For violence and thievery. Take your pick. That kind of kid will stop at nothing. We're talking about the harsh realities now you know. Not boys like ... you know, like Mark, or Ben. These are strays. Wild kids. Feral kids. That's what! With no sense of ...'

'But kids,' her mother interrupted. 'Still kids.'

'Desperadoes. Not like the kids at home you used to take in, if that's what you're thinking, Mum. You probably believe you can save him like all those other waifs and strays. But that was a long time ago. And that was in the country. This is the city and these kids—these kids—well, they're damaged goods.'

'Precisely, Jane. A perfect description for that young boy. Already damaged by life. By too little love. I think I can help him. That's all—just by talking.'

'Some kids are beyond help. Beyond redemption. Can't you understand that? Beyond it! Not only that, some of them, probably most of them, don't really want to be helped. And least of all by the likes of someone like you! Sure he'll take your food, your money. Then he'll disappear with some of your things. Back on the streets looking for thrills. I know their type—those kids knocking around, they *like* it. Don't you understand? They like being down-and-outs!'

'That's where you're wrong, Jane. Nobody likes being down-and-out.'

'They think people like you are suckers—and quite frankly, Mum, so do I ... And I won't have the likes of him coming to my house.'

'If he does come here, Jane—which I doubt—it will be to knock at my door up the back. You said the flat was to be mine. So if I understood you correctly, it will be my house and not yours he comes to. And if he does, he'll be more than welcome.'

Their raised voices had brought Ben to the kitchen. He stood in the doorway, dismayed.

Mother and daughter stared at each other, then Jane turned away. She'd said over and over that her mother should look on the flat up the back as her own home. To come and go as she pleased. To have what visitors she pleased. But a street kid! She knew her mother's intentions were good, of course. She knew how many kids her mother had helped in the past. She had a way of talking to them that earned their respect. Just like she talked to Ben. But this was too much. They'd have to have it out when Ben went to bed, once and for all.

'Is the bad boy coming here?' Ben's eyes were large.

'No,' Jane and Iris said together.

'No bad boy will ever come here,' the old woman added quietly.

22

Pursuit

Robbie was running for his life. Down a lane that led into another lane. This maze of a city seemed filled with lanes like this: dirty, dark, with doorways that could leap out at you and swallow you up. He needed somewhere now that could swallow him up. But where? Where?

The thudding sound in his ears was not the pounding of his own feet on the gritty pavement; the huge man who'd lunged out at him was in pursuit. He'd come from nowhere in that shop, almost caught him with his big outreaching hands, and then lost him to the darkness of the lane. But not for long, for he was gaining on him now.

He heard the panting directly behind him and a voice thick with anger, 'Filthy, sleazy, little jerk—I'll ...'

Robbie had no time to catch his breath, to look left or right. He ran straight ahead into blackness.

'... get you.'

Had he dreamt this once? A narrow, dark place and running and running. Cavities opening up under his feet. The road narrowing and holes widening, either side an abyss. Hands reaching out through the dark for him. Big thick hands grasping for his fleeing back. Hands that would snap him like a rotten stick.

Coming to get you. Like a game he'd played as a little kid. *Coming, coming to get you.*

There was a cluster of bins up ahead now where the lane forked. He'd seen things in the movies about chases, oh, dozens of times. He hurled himself in among the bins scattering them across the roadway. He heard the steps behind falter, a fall and a stream of abuse, as he ducked out of sight down another laneway.

No one behind him now. It had worked just like it did in the movies, like a charm. Given him some respite!

But what did they do in movies when they came to a dead end? The roadway went no further. Not lane into lane or lane into passageway or lane into stairs, as it did so often round here. There were just blank brick walls on two sides, with windows way way up, and a high paling fence.

Caught like a rat in a trap!

In the movies they'd climb up the wall or fence, quick as a flash the stuntman'd be up it, over it and away.

Robbie knew he was in for the hiding of his life—well before the police came to take him away to God knows what hell.

Coming to get you. Coming to get you. Like a game

FERAL KID o

he'd played as a little kid. I'll get you.

Well he wouldn't be got!

The top of the fence was high. Double the height of a normal fence. It was edged with lattice. Nice bits of wood with handholds and toeholds way up there. There was a battered bin in the gutter. He grabbed it and upturned it, but directly above there was nothing to grab onto—only smooth wood. He couldn't reach the top and the latticework even with the bin under him. And the big man had turned into this lane now. He could hear his pounding feet again.

He'd had it. In a moment grasping hands would tear him down, hammy fists would punch into his face unmercifully and heavy boots would kick him to the ground, kick him senseless. He knew it.

There was a mass of flowers growing at the other end of the fence. Big puffy loops of white starry stuff trailing down. If it were thick enough under the flowers, if it were strong enough ... He dragged the bin beneath it. At first leap the flowers came away in his hand, sticky light stuff which he crushed in rage and fear.

Don't turn round, you silly prat. Don't look in his pig eyes. Do it. Get up there. Do it now.

The second desperate leap took him up further into the vine. As his pursuer lunged towards him, Robbie's hand closed round a thick coil, seasons old, which held fast. He swung his feet and body swung up and into a mass of flowers and crisscross vine on lattice. Right up to the top.

121

He saw what was on the other side before the man below called triumphantly. 'Go on, ya jerk. Jump and break you're bleedin' neck. If you come down this side I'll break it for you!'

He was still in a trap. The high fence was perched on the edge of a cliff. And way down, in a pool of light, was the backyard of a terrace house. He looked over into the abyss. Fooled himself, hadn't he? Well ,what now idiot? What in the hell now? If he jumped he'd break his neck. He looked back, down into the red face of fury. And if he didn't ...

The man shook the fence. 'Go on jump, you little rat—or I'll push the bleedin' thing down,' and he threw his burly weight against it.

There was a crack, and Robbie lost his hold on the flimsy lattice. He didn't need to make the decision to jump: he was going ...

He'd fallen in dreams too. In dreams the sickening sensation had gone on and on. But one second he'd been perched at the top of that fence and then the next he'd been falling down, down through space. He braced himself for the impact of the earth. For shock and shattering pain and numbness. Maybe for the blank nothingness of his death ...

But there was no pain. Things snapped and gave, but not his body. He was winded, confused, but he was alive, all right. A thick grove of palms had broken his fall. He seemed to bounce the last few metres from branch to bushes, and then down to the earth.

His shoulder hit the ground hard, but he was on his feet. He was in a mini jungle, against the edge of a cliff in someone's backyard.

And it had not gone unnoticed. Three or four young people, yelling their shock and concern, were heading out of a pool of light near the house towards him. Up above, in the dark world of the back lanes, there was the sound of sirens.

Perhaps an angel had saved him, he thought, ready to face the people coming towards him. He could already see through the bushes that the house, a big terrace, sat fatly across the land. There was no way out except right through the house. Out of the jungle and into their arms. Perhaps the angel was still around.

It was a girl who reached him first. 'Are you all right? Oh my God, we saw you fall ...' She sounded near tears. Their eyes met in the half dark.

Then behind her came two young men. 'Hell, mate, are you OK?'

Blinking and dishevelled in the glare of their lights, he thought he must look like a fugitive. It seemed there was a party going on, because there were other young people, all very dressed up. Their mouths hung open in amazement. In a moment they would grab him, in minutes he'd be bundled off to a gaol, like the one Pale had told him about. But right now, no one moved.

He sprang up onto the verandah leading to the house and one of the boys grabbed him roughly by the shoulder.

'Listen you—just what the hell d'you think you're doing?'

But the girl he'd first seen yelled, 'Leave him alone, Justin.'

'There's something going on up top. Police cars. Can't you hear?'

'I said leave him alone.' The ice in her tone made the boy fall back.

'Don't be an idiot. He's probably a ...'

'You can go through there,' and she indicated the back door. She held it open for him!

'Don't be crazy—don't let him——' He heard the chorus of voices behind him. Through the door and down the hall, he didn't lose a moment. Maybe it was a trick. There'd be a security grille at the other end and they'd bail him up again—but the front door opened under his grasp and he was out in the street again.

Up top there was a commotion, but down here was a safe darkness to hide in. He moved swiftly out of the street and threaded his way through another laneway. This one wasn't filthy and squalid, only untidy and suburban with its vines and garage doors. He scaled a lowish fence with ease and found his way through a side door into a garage. Had to have somewhere to stay until it all calmed down out there. Had to have a rest.

A car had claimed nearly all the space in here. Oh God no, it was a Porsche—wouldn't you know it! A bleedin' Porsche, of all cars! And they'd probably think he'd come to steal it. Don't touch the bleedin' thing or an alarm would shriek for sure. He looked round. In the dark he could make out beach chairs at one end of the garage. He made his way carefully around the car without so much as brushing it. He undid the folding chair, and curled up. It was lovely having canvas under him, and not cold in here at all.

He'd have to go on soon, but a little shut eye now, then at first light he'd leave. His body was aching, specially his shoulder, and he thought maybe he'd hurt himself in the fall more than he'd imagined. He could put up with that. It was the prospect of the day that terrified him.

He shut his eyes to sleep, but he kept seeing the big dark fall the other side of the fence, the red screwed-up face of the man and the white pretty face of the girl. And then the viaduct and Pale's mother cat and then the little—no!

Pale was gone. And Mandy was gone too. Just like everyone he'd ever known was gone. He was a piece of shit in this big don't-care city, a scrap of bleedin' newsprint. He was lost in this soddin' place he'd wanted so badly to get to. A million bleedin' people maybe. But he was alone in somebody's chair in somebody's garage in nowhere land. He was a nothing and a nobody with no place to go.

Then he thought of the old woman for a moment. Tears sprang to his eyes as he realised the impossibility of going to her. 'Oh, I've just been part of a robbery and a bashing. But don't be frightened. I just want to hide out for a few days, and you said if I ever needed help ...'

He could imagine her scared eyes. Like the people at that party. All of them scared witless. All of them except the girl. The pale girl who'd stood up to the jerk in the poncy shirt who'd tried to grab him. That girl had a bit of spunk, she'd held open the door and said quite loud and quite definite, 'You can go through there'. Why had she done that? He'd like to know why she'd done that when all the others were against her.

Just like Pale had helped the poor stray cat, she'd helped a stray. Well thanks for nothing, silly cow.

He wished he'd fallen down the bleedin' cliff on to concrete and killed himself outright. It'd be all over, wouldn't it? They'd have gathered round him, so shocked, all those posh kids. They'd have been glad when they saw who he was. Nobody. But she'd have been sad, the girl. He would have been carried out with a white sheet over him and she'd probably have cried like anything.

Yeah, the fat man should've shaken him out of his tree like a dog shaking a rat. Shaking it to death. Or he should've fallen properly—backwards. Cracked his thick skull open on their fancy brickwork. And then he wouldn't have had to think what he could bleedin' do next ...

It took him a few moments to remember, as it often did, when he opened his eyes. He was stiff, and there was a curious red glow up the walls. All warm and rosy, the light, and at the little high window leaves moving softly. Green as one thing and the dawn sky behind. He rubbed his eyes. What was this red smear, shiny and vast in front of him? And where in the hell was he?

The garage of course. He moved in the chair, but his shoulder seemed to want to stay behind. He rubbed it. Nah—not broken, just bruised, for sure. He stood up awkwardly, brushing against the car. He froze, but there was no terrible sound alerting them in there. No alarm at all. He leaned forward on the car, relaxed for a moment. Could've broken into it and slept on a padded leather seat!

Nearly morning and the proper people, the people who had letterboxes and shiny red cars with padded leather seats would be up and about soon. They'd call the police if they so much as caught a glimpse of him here.

He needed to pee badly. Not outside. They might stare out windows, do exercises or something on their bloody balconies. No, he'd do it here, piss against the tyres of their fancy car like a dog. If he had the time he'd do a number on the door too, like he'd seen Pale do. A fancy Merc parked at the Cross. Quick as flash, just walking by, Pale had scraped it one end to the other with a twenty cent piece. A nice deep groove. And you didn't even see him do it.

'God, Pale,' he'd said, looking back at the scar along the shiny surface.

'Give the jerks something to think about,' Pale had said, 'something to spend their lousy millions on.'

Well, he understood all that now. With the smell of urine rising up in his nostrils he hated this red car as he hated the people in this house. Hated them and feared them, as he knew they hated and feared him.

He let himself out into the lane. Already there was that hum in the air that meant the city was coming to life. And the light this morning seemed extra bright. He ran his hand through his hair, feeling it stiff and greasy. *Well, don't just stand here waiting for breakfast on a tray. Think, think, you jerk, about what you do, where you go next. Go on dimwit, think!*

'Natasha, your mother and I have had a long talk about your behaviour on Saturday night.'

She dreaded the talks she and her father had in the car as he ferried her to school on the way to his office in town. Even when he was in a good mood, there often seemed to be a reprimand of some kind.

'Your mother's most upset, as you know. She can't understand why you refuse to give a reason for helping that boy.'

'Not that again,' Natasha thought grimly, staring at the line of traffic ahead.

'I thought I'd let you know we've decided to phone all the parents of the young people present at your party, to explain that you were not yourself, that ...'

'Oh Dad, that's hardly necessary.'

'Most necessary,' her father said coldly, 'though difficult to say why you allowed—no, helped—this boy to escape, right though our house! When he'd just bashed and tried to rob an elderly man!'

'I don't think so!'

'The police think so. What makes you think any other way?'

She was going to remain silent, as she did when her mother harangued her for hours on end. But she saw him again in her mind's eye, the young boy blinking into the strung-up lights of her party, remembered distinctly the look of bewilderment, and fear and helplessness.

'His eyes, they were—well—they were honest!' she burst out.

Her father snorted, 'His eyes!'

'How would you feel, how would anyone—to make a jump like that, all of us there staring at him, being chased, scared?'

'It's unfortunate that some children have a tough time of it. I know all about that, as you well know. But after a more than difficult childhood, I got on with my life. Made choices. And so has he. You can let yourself be trapped by circumstances or not. I think you'll find he's a bad boy, a very poor type.'

'I don't care what anyone else thinks, he needed help,' she said stubbornly, 'and he isn't bad.'

'Natasha, I don't know if you begin to understand how hard your mother and I have had to work for you.

To buy a house in the right suburb. To send you to the right school. To make sure you had the right friends. And then you go and make friends with a—well—with a street fighter.'

She'd heard all this so many times before it shouldn't really make her angry, but she felt the usual fury rising. What was the use of saying that she hadn't made friends with him, but that she might like to ...?

'You're to apologise to your mother and think about a reasonable explanation she can give for your behaviour while you're at it!'

There was no possible answer when he spoke like this. As the big car slid to a stop outside the right school and she was forced to give him the dutiful goodbye kiss, he had the last word.

'And no more parties for quite some time. Until you learn some of life's important lessons. Until you learn to behave in a responsible and sensible manner.'

Responsible, sensible. She trudged up the school drive, past the knots of girls talking and laughing. She couldn't get the face of the boy out of her mind. In the cool of the large hallway she heard the voice of her form mistress, a favourite teacher of hers.

'Natasha, could you step into my office in about five minutes please. Your mother has just phoned the school and she seems very worried about you. I think we should have a little talk.'

No matter what they said, her mother, her father, even the shrink her parents had sent her to once when she'd disobeyed them, Natasha was sure that on Saturday night, helping that boy had been the right thing. Having some pity for him as well as some respect, considering the desperate jump he'd made into their garden, was right. She thought now of a quote they'd discussed in an English class only a week back, something about 'the milk of human kindness'. That's what he'd needed, for he was liked a trapped animal in more ways than one.

But as Natasha made her way to the office for another talk she dreaded, thinking of that boy with the beautiful face and the big scared eyes, she realised something quite curious. If he, the wild boy, was trapped by his circumstances, then so was she. Oh, in quite another way, but so was she.

23
Hiding

Funny, he'd chosen a place that had spooked him so badly just looking inside it. He'd been here two days now. In the end it was the only place he could think of in the whole of the city where he might be safe.

The reservoir was still empty, thank God, though it smelled dank. Water came oozing out of the massive wall behind him, and up out of the uneven stone floor he lay on. He'd spread his jacket, but he was already wet through. And he knew he couldn't stay here like this much longer. It had been filled with water for a hundred years! It was no wonder that even when it was emptied, it was so thick and damp down here. A hell hole of his own choice!

On the first night his shoulder had ached so intensely it kept waking him. He had come to each time with a start, for the blackness was thick and unrelenting. He had to remind himself not to cry out with surprise. Remind himself of where he was and why he was here.

Remind himself to look carefully, carefully just over there to the left and way, way up to the vaulted ceiling for the airhole. A nice, comforting, round airhole that let in not only air. There were pale streaks of light that let him know he was still in the world. Not buried in hell or something in absolute dark.

On the second night there'd been the rats! He'd sure yelled out then.

Workers came into the place during the day. That's how he knew roughly what time it was. The airholes, maybe twenty of them studded all round the place, let in the very first light of early morning so that he saw that night was over at last. The workers would soon swing back the heavy door they'd put up at the far side, then he'd hear their voices, cheerful in the gloom, as the roughly strung lights came on way up near the ceiling. They were busy mending the far wall, and there were shouts and sometimes laughter, the sound of machinery over there all day.

Nobody ever came up here, beside the thick brick wall that divided the huge reservoir in two. He felt quite safe for the moment. It was when the machines whirred to a stop, the string of lights went out and the late afternoon sun streamed down the airholes like golden light from a holy picture, that he felt worst of all.

When the far wall was mended, which it must be in the next few days (perhaps even the next few hours), they would close off the gateway they'd made, fill it with bricks and cement and stone and seal it off permanently. So the water could pour back in and stay brimming almost up to the top for another hundred years.

He had to be out of here by the time they did that. He and the rats! And it would happen soon. Though he went over and over it in his mind, there seemed to be no where he could go once he left here. No where at all.

He imagined Pale's face distorted and angry, as the police dragged him away. This sight haunted Robbie while he hid out in the dank, resounding reservoir by day. And haunted him when he tried to sleep through the damp, nightmarish nights. Pale'd go up the river for a few years, probably, and here was he scot-free. Free as the breeze—well, sort of—but scared witless and wet through.

Another thought occurred to him. 'Have to really watch it,' he said out loud, thinking of the massive pumps he had seen, and how they would suddenly begin the refilling. The water would shoot inside here with such force that he might never get past those pumps, might drown trying to get past them. They were positioned on the hideout side of the wall, quite near!

'Nah, I'd have lots of time,' he comforted himself. 'Lots.' They'd have to seal up the gaping hole in the wall over there first, to hold the water in, wouldn't they? And that couldn't happen overnight. Or could it?

'Nah, there's machinery scattered every whichway,' he said out loud again. 'They wouldn't leave machinery inside.' He'd be safe until they started moving it out.

But he'd have to get out of here soon. He'd worked through the chocolate bars and chips he'd brought with him. And anyway, two days had passed now. Pale would be locked up. But then there was the thought of Lal and 'his friend', out there stalking around, looking, asking, waiting.

What if Pale had told Lal about the reservoir?

There'd been no money for Lal the rock spider. A botched job and his fault. Lal could kill. Well, look what he'd done to Pale's kitten. For what reason, he'd never know—never want to know. Lal might be coming after him, looking, asking, waiting, right now.

And if he did leave this underground place, just where could he go, eh? He'd been over this a hundred times, and still no place occurred to him. Pale knew about the squat and Pale would maybe tell the police. They might make him dob in people. He'd heard they sometimes made you do that. The squat was out. Pale knew the City Mission, too, and every other damn place that Mandy had told him about. There was nowhere in this city that Pale didn't know about. Maybe Lal as well. 'And don't you ever try to do the dirty on me. Or you'll know what for!' The words went over and over in his mind.

Well, he'd done the dirty, hadn't he? And the old guy had pressed the alarm. God, bells had gone off and a young man had jumped out of nowhere and grabbed hold of Pale, looking ready to kill him. And people, people had come from every direction!

It was funny, unexpected, what had happened there in the shop. It replayed through his mind as he lay in the dark. Sometimes he just couldn't stop it.

The pink, round, unprotected head.
The mild rim of the old man's hair.
The crazy old-time music.
You made me, you made me
The glint of the metal
under fluorescence.
Pale's raised hand,
and the long pause.
love you, I didn't
Pink, round, soft, shiny.
want to do it, I didn't
How long, how long,
could this moment ...
want to do it
Do it Pale, sod you! Do it!
Do it now!
Unexpected, singing violence.
and all the time
A taste of blood
between his teeth,
in his mouth.
I knew it, I didn't
Smash him now!
really want to do it
Do it! Do it

You know you made me
love you

Was it him or had it been Pale? Who had made that unearthly sound, a wailing, warning cry? One of them had, the moment before the gun had come crashing down towards the pink skull. A moment that meant the blow was deflected. It must have been him, because Pale cursed him, then hit out at the old man again. Too late. The bell was already ringing.

Ringing to wake the dead. Bell, voices, cries, curses, hallway, laneway, darkness, fear. Blood was spilling down his forehead but the old man had turned, to put up his hands, not before Pale brought down the gun again and again.

Not before Robbie had seen the man's dark surprised eyes. He'd run then, run for his life.

Maybe, though, he'd dreamt about that fall down the cliff face. His shoulder told him no. He'd arrived, an uninvited guest at that party. How strange the girl, so proper in her blue dress with her perfect blue eyes and her perfect blue headband, had held open the door for him. Had let him go, and by doing so had made him go on.

The idea of the empty reservoir had come to him as dawn broke over the city. In the lane outside the place with the red Porsche, he'd remembered it. Where was the darkest, quietest, most secret place in this hellhole? Hellhole! That was it. Pale's reservoir. They'd never find him there. Never ever. Why hadn't he thought of it before?

There was a shop near the park, too, open twenty-four hours. He could buy something to eat and drink and then he could hide himself good and proper. It had only taken ten minutes to reach the park and buy his stuff, then another ten to climb inside the place. He didn't have Pale's strength to prise open the door easily, but he'd managed to move it enough to squeeze through. But, God, it was a scary bleedin' hole of a place. 'It could be worse,' he made himself say.

'Who's there?' his voice was thin, but it echoed through the place. 'Who?'

Something had fallen, over there in the dark. Or rather there was a scattering. Then he heard the scampering and the unmistakable squeaks. A rat. No, rats. He closed his hand over the brick at the top of the pile he'd stashed right beside him. 'Get. Geeet,' he called, and heaved the brick in their direction.

Oh God, he couldn't stay here another night and let them come and run right over his body! He couldn't let that happen again. He'd woken last night and somehow been aware, in the utter blackness, of a living thing nearby. Something was breathing near his ear, he was sure. And something else was stealthily, furtively moving up his leg.

At first he'd thought by the weight of it that it must be a cat. But there was a noise near his other ear. An unmistakable noise. And another near his hand. And that scampering sound. He realised he was probably surrounded by them. By rats as big as cats. Attracted by the food he'd brought in, crumbs of chocolate, maybe, still on the ground. Or the warm human smell of him. They were gathering round him. 'Ahhhhh!' He'd jumped to his feet and called so loudly they'd taken off in all directions. He'd heard them all go scattering on their scrabbly little feet, all over the floor in every direction, and even up the wall behind him. He'd heard them all right.

He'd stood for the remainder of the night. Calling out to keep them away. Once he'd called his nan's name, he felt so lonely and scared. But that only made him feel little, like Mel, and really bad. He sang, though, and they didn't come back, the little jerks. He let himself sink down on the floor to sleep only when a sickly dawn light appeared. At least the daylight carried off those creatures of the night. But he was a creature of the night himself now.

He'd have to get away from here, couldn't face another night with the rats. Yet he didn't, couldn't, move. He sat miserably staring into the dark, listening.

It had been almost too easy for him to get out of the shop, but he'd heard Pale's foul mouth, cursing him.

'If ever I get locked up again, I reckon I'll do myself in,' Pale had said that night at the viaduct. Drunk from the beer he kept swigging, he'd talked and talked.

'I couldn't take it again. The way they get at you on
the inside. No way. I'd go mad I would. Bleedin' soddin'
mad! I could never be locked up again! Not with the
screws the way they are. And the other kids. You know
what happens to new boys in there. After you've been
raped, that is. Let me tell you about the first time you go
in a place like that one, and what they do to you besides
that ...'

And now Pale would be locked up in there again, and
it was all his fault.

He shifted, feeling the wetness soaking through his
jeans. He felt like Pale's swimming friend, what was his
name—Ritch, the one who'd been so frightened of
turning into a skeleton down here. Maybe he *was* down
here. Maybe Pale had pulled up the rope one day and
left the poor little kid to drown. To turn into a skeleton.
The way Pale had talked about the kid, frightening him
like that. The way Pale liked to have power over people.
Robbie was sick with the thought of it. Of bones in a
pile in some corner of the place, Ritch's skeleton. It felt
like death in here. Like someone maybe had died down
here. Yeah, it felt like death all right.

He felt tears sliding down his cheeks. Hell, he'd
promised himself he wouldn't cry. Knew if he started
then he wouldn't be able to stop the bad thoughts.
Wouldn't be able to hold on. He wiped his eyes, his
cheeks, his nose with his sleeve, angrily, and made
himself lie down. 'I'll go to sleep,' he told himself, but
the wetness and the cold were worse than ever, now

he'd stretched out. God, he could have been floating down a bleedin' river with all this water.

And then it came to him. An amazing thought. A thrilling thought. So simple and so perfect, he actually smiled in the darkness. He knew now just what he was going to do.

24
Going Home

Iris was standing by the duck pond. There was the usual scuffle up the banks of the more daring or hungrier birds, and the waddling onslaught of the geese, already stepping it out over the grass. She stared out at the still surface of the lake and thought of busy, swirling water. The wide, wild, hurrying swirl of a big old river. The thought tugged at her so hard that for a moment she almost lost her balance. For with the river she saw her house, dilapidated and empty in the overgrown garden, clear as day, with the morning breaking over the river. The mist, the bending reeds, the paddocks full of cane and the birds getting ready for the day.

She felt a sharp pain in her heart. Not the jagged, unexpected hospital pain that came now and then. This one was quite different in quality, but just as intense. It was the unrelenting pain of homesickness that made her whole body feel lost and far away.

'I'll go home,' she said to herself, surprised and a

little breathless at the simplicity of the idea. 'That's it. I'll go home right away.' She tossed her bagful of bread, in whole slices, into the reedy waters by the edge, causing a commotion among the smaller birds. The street boy had suggested it to her, hadn't he? Right here in the park by this very pond, he'd said in that quiet voice of his, 'You should go home. To the river. You should go anyway.' Well, he was right, that wild kid. Not so wild after all.

She thought of the shambly house with its sagging verandahs and ill-fitting doors, with its out-of-date kitchen and its creaking wooden floors, its wide hallway and its bright glass-panelled front door. Home. Why hadn't she decided to do this weeks ago—as soon as she felt well again? Why had she allowed herself to become a burden on Jane? She'd only brought unhappiness to Jane's home, she reflected. There was no life for her here. Her life was up there, up north, in the warmth and the peacefulness. But what about Ben? She'd miss the little fellow such a lot. Ben could visit her on holidays and Jane, too, if only she would ...

'I'm hoping you won't feel annoyed, Jane,' Iris began when she found her daughter in the kitchen, beginning to cook dinner. 'Specially after all you've done for me.'

Jane spoke in an irritated manner. 'What is this after-all-I've-done nonsense?'

'I'm going home,' the old woman announced.

'But that's out of the question, Mum,' Jane shrugged,

turning back to her chopping board. 'You're being impulsive, Mum.'

'Not impulsive. I've been thinking about home for weeks. And today I had such a strange feeling over there in the park, such a strong feeling, almost as if I was in the big old river. You know, out there in the middle where you're forced to go with the current.'

'This is silly talk.' Jane began slicing carrots again with quick, nervous movements.

'Not silly. The feeling was so very strong I knew in an instant that I'd have to go. That it was very, very important for me to go!'

Her mother's tone made Jane turn to face her.

'Like the premonition I had about Mark. About not letting him join that team. About not letting him go with that older boy in the car. Only I didn't do anything about that. Maybe it wouldn't have made any difference if I'd stopped Mark. But maybe it would have. Anyway, that's the kind of feeling I had today. Only this time I can do something about it. There's still time.'

'Oh, Mum!' Jane always felt wretched when any mention of Mark was made. Didn't know what to say.

'I've got to do it, Jane.'

'But you can't go back to that lonely place,' Jane insisted.

'Look, if you want to move somewhere else close by, I'd understand, Mum.'

'I've been more lonely here,' the old woman said, 'than I've ever been at home. Not that I'm saying it's your fault, Jane. More my own—but that's the truth, dear.'

The truth was, having her mother so close it had been much more difficult than Jane had expected. And now Ben seemed filled with all kinds of ideas that were undoubtedly her mother's. Frightening him when he was far too young with things about global warming, about forests being cut down. There was a lot of truth in what she said—that was the trouble. But what was the point of worrying a small boy? Now that his father wasn't here and she got home so late from work, he was spending a lot of time with Iris.

'I've been *called* home,' the old woman said firmly. 'Clarence River home.'

Another one of her mother's foolish ideas.

'Called? By whom, Mum?'

'Let's just say the river called me, Jane.'

'Oh, Mum, really.'

'Well, I'm going.'

'What about your heart condition then?'

'What about it? That'll follow me now wherever I go,' Iris said calmly, 'and to tell the truth I think life is better for me up there than down here. All this traffic and noise and no air—enough to make anyone's heart condition worse, if you ask me. I won't ever get used to a city at my age.'

'You must know it could be downright dangerous for you to be alone—so far away from hospitals.'

'I'd rather die up there by my old river than in any

noisy hospital, if I must die. But I'm not planning on going for some time yet.'

'Of course not,' Jane said, 'but ...'

'No buts, I'm going, and that's that. Let's face it, Jane. The experiment's failed. You don't really like my being here any more than I do.'

'Mum, don't talk like that.'

'Let's be honest for once.'

Jane was quiet. Her mother was speaking the truth, but how could she admit it. 'I'll make us some tea,' she said quietly, 'and we'll talk some more.'

'About my travel arrangements,' Iris insisted. 'It's OK, Jane—don't take it to heart. An experiment is just that. To see if it works. And this one didn't. We love each other, of course we do,' and she placed her finely wrinkled hand over her daughter's smooth brown one. 'But not so much on a day-to-day basis. There, I've said it.'

'Mum!' Jane was shocked, couldn't think what to say. 'What if Ben's listening to this? Anyway, it's not true ...'

'Being here, you know, I've come to know young Ben really well. And that's wonderful. He reminds me so much of you at the same age.'

'Oh, Mum, it's not that I ...'

'You and Ben, should come up and see me. Not talk about it as you've done for years. Really come to stay at Rochedale. The boy would love the river, all kids do. And I'd like him to see me in my own territory. And it was your territory, too, for that matter.'

Jane poured the tea, her mind in a whirl. If she agreed with her mother it would mean she had failed as a daughter, wouldn't it? Admit that you didn't like your own mother living so close! It was dreadful. And yet something told her there was a chance that she might get to know her mother in a quite different way if she could be as honest as Iris was being.

She looked up to see her mother smiling at her. Sometimes she could be so ... so ... Oh, what the hell, admit it, Jane. Admit your mother is right and you're wrong, and maybe we'll get somewhere.

'You're right,' she said at last. 'We'll look into the travel arrangements for you.'

'I'd like to leave straight away.'

'Oh, Mum, please give it a few days.'

'Well, no longer. I've got to get going, Jane. Somehow, now I've made up my mind, it seems urgent. I'm going to take the train.'

'But why not fly? It's such a long haul all the way up there by train.'

'I love that train journey—all the stations are like old friends. And getting off at Lismore, it'll be like ...' she stopped herself saying it'd be like heaven and said instead, '... old times.'

'We'll have to arrange for somebody to meet you.'

'Plenty who'll do that. Mr Armani, if I phone him.'

'Mr Armani! He's not still driving at his age! God, he must be ...'

'An excellent driver at eighty-two Jane. Beats the hell out of a lot of drivers I've seen around this place.'

Jane was surprised at her mother's language, but not at her loyalty to old friends. She smiled. 'If you say so, Mum.'

'I do.'

They drank their tea in their first companionable silence in weeks. She'd never understand her mother, not really. But Jane admired her determination to do things. She'd decided to go home now that she was feeling so well again. And come hell or high water, go home she would.

'Jane—there's something else I want to say before I leave. So I might as well say it here and now.'

What was this? Jane looked worried. It was sure to be something unpleasant.

'You should tell Ben the truth about his father,' she said. 'About Paul.'

Jane was silent a moment, looking down into her teacup. Unpleasant but necessary. 'I've been thinking that for a while, Mum. But I don't know how to. I mean, how do you say to a boy his age that his father isn't coming home ever again? That he's decided to live in London forever and ...'

'Begin by saying just that.'

'He'll be so upset.'

'Even more if he thinks you're keeping the truth from him. Look, Jane, Ben is a good little kid, and I think if you tell him he'll adjust to the idea. He can get in contact with his father then, and they can talk about it. Even make plans. There are lots of kids who have had to do the same.'

'I'll think about it,' Jane said uncertainly. But later that evening when Ben had gone to bed, she did think about it and she knew that her mother was right. And she was glad something had at last been said out in the open. She had to face the truth of it herself, difficult though it was. Ben should know the truth about his father, too, and she should tell him soon.

Maybe when her mother was back up north and settled, in a month or two, maybe she should take Ben for a long visit. Maybe it would be nice to revisit her old haunts. Even to talk to neighbours like Mrs Armani and some of her old schoolfriends, the ones who had stayed and made farming their life. It was a rather lovely part of the world. She'd had a wonderful childhood up there with the river so nearby. So free, and so much to do as a little kid. Much better than poor old Ben here in the city where there were too many dangers. Maybe she should think seriously about life in a country town herself. No, that was not for her. Not now. But good long holidays were certainly a possibility.

It was quite true what her mother had said about Ben. The boy would love it, go mad over the river ...

Calm and wakeful in her bed later that night, Iris pictured her old home bathed in late afternoon light— and the river glittering behind it. Yes, it would be late afternoon when she got there. The garden would look overgrown, of course, but lovely with the wattle out. She'd have a lot to do once she got there—the place would need a good going over. A lot to do. She knew she should get her rest, for the next few days would be busy ones.

Newcastle, Taree, Coffs Harbour, Lismore ... She fell asleep reciting the names of the towns on the way home.

25
The River

He'd get out of this city once and for all. He'd do it first thing in the morning.

'Nothing much to pack,' he said out loud, smiling at his own joke, smiling because this thought that filled his head was so wonderful he could hardly keep from yelling it out into the vault of the empty reservoir.

He'd go down to the station. Central wasn't far from here. A fifteen minute walk maybe. He'd wait around until he could get on a train heading north. No trouble hiding on a train. He'd done it plenty of times going to and from Campbelltown.

He'd go up north. Get the hell out of this city. Way up north to the river. The one he'd dreamed about. Only it was *her* river he'd go to—the old lady's. Not his nan's in that town in Italy, that was a plane ride away. Not the river with the old, old, houses and the palaces and things that he'd see one day. Sure as hell he'd see.

No, he'd go to a river much closer, much easier to reach for now. He'd ask somebody on the train about her river, the Clarence—that's what she'd said. The Clarence way up north where it was warm. And he knew if he did that—well—somehow, some crazy way or other, everything would be all right. He could hear it singing as he could hear that voice that had long ago soothed and promised. He didn't know why it hadn't occurred to him before. The idea of the river. The river. It'd be OK if he could just get up there, he knew it!

What was the name of the town? Her town? He couldn't think what it was just now, but he'd remember it in a minute. Sure to. And he'd cut out of that town and follow the road to the river to her house. He was certain he could find her house. She'd given such a good description of the road. Even mentioned the name of it, off some big highway. It'd come to him, he was sure of it once he was on the train heading north. And he'd cut along the road until he saw it.

He lay back on his jacket and suddenly it seemed as if he were lying in a soft bed in a generous darkness. He'd have to rest so he could get out first thing in the morning. Get out of this city forever. Well, maybe later, when things were better, he'd come back to find Mandy. To say sorry to her. He'd work it all out once he got up there to the river. Mandy should get out of this place, too. Away from her boyfriend. It'd be all right. He lay back and he stared upwards feeling peaceful. There wasn't a sound. Not even the tiniest scrabbling of a rat in the dark.

But there seemed to be a map hanging in the air. Not Nan's old map, the one she'd haul out from the drawer lots of times to show him when his dad wasn't about. The river, the mountains, the cities. Her town. Her river. Her sea. Her place. That map was blurred with too much use, frayed at the edges with so much looking at it. Not hers, but a map of another kind. Like a great glowing video it was, like one of the pinball machines that took you places. This was a map of a town and a road and a river that he could trace with his finger in the air. He could see that map so clearly, it was as if it was really there, and he hadn't taken anything neither. He could trace the way he'd take, right to her house.

The old wooden house wasn't hanging up there conveniently like the map though. But it was in his head, just like she'd told him. Big old run-down place, cream and green he thought, with the wire gate and the name on it. What was it? Yep, he could remember that all right. Rochedale.

Of course she wouldn't be there, he told himself. She didn't live in Rochedale any more. She lived here in the city with her daughter. The one she didn't seem to like much, and with her grandson who she did like. But he couldn't get rid of an image of her there, no matter how hard he tried.

Over and over, in the hours before he finally fell asleep, he imagined himself opening the front gate. And as if in a dream he imagined himself going up the front path, through all the weeds and things. Going up this path to the sagging front steps. He imagined an old door with coloured glass panels. Reaching out, he'd knock quite hard and quite loud.

And that knocking which he could hear in his head right now, that knocking wouldn't echo through an empty house. It wouldn't, because he knew he'd hear the sound of someone's footsteps inside. And then the old glass-panelled door would open and she'd be there, the old lady from the park, to welcome him into her house near her river. And he'd go right on inside. Well, that was the dream anyway. And even if it didn't work out like that, it'd be better than rotting here.

Robbie couldn't wait until morning. The chill was so bad when he woke in the early hours he thought he'd go down to railway station straight away.

'Goodbye deadbeat rats! Goodbye sleazeballs,' he said as he made his way uncertainly across the floor towards the chink of light that announced the makeshift door and the way out.

Outside, under a waning moon, the air seemed warm. His clothes would dry in no time.

'She won't be up there, up north,' he said to himself as he passed the houses crouching beside the park with their large backyards and little flats out the back for grandmothers.

'She won't be there because she's here. But the house will be just like she said. And the river.'

If he could only get to the house, he knew it would be

like coming home. Simple as that. The thought carried him effortlessly through the city towards Central.

'Have to, have to,' his swift feet pounded out over the city pavements, across the city roads and on and on towards the station. He had to make it, that's all he knew. And no one would stop him! He glanced fearfully around the empty streets and quickened his pace. Ten more minutes and he'd be at the safety of the station, where he'd find the train that'd take him away. He had to make it, that's all he knew. He would make it. 'Make it, make it,' his feet were light again and he was fast.

And he'd find Mandy, wherever she was. Funny that, in going away from her he was sure he could find her. Maybe when he did, she could come up north, too. They were linked now, he and Mandy. Didn't he have her sign, the frog that meant good luck, that bright green fella the old lady had admired, tattooed on his arm forever. It might just as well have said 'Mandy Forever'. It meant the same thing. And it wasn't as silly as it sounded, Mandy up north, away from the Cross, the gritty streets, the cruel faces and garish lights. Away from people like Lal and Pale. Pale. Oh, God, Pale! Maybe he'd even find out where they'd put him. But the thought of that frightened him. Maybe not. Amanda, Mandy first. He even let himself think of Melanie.

The tall sandstone clocktower of the station was in sight when a police car slid up out of the darkness beside him.

'You, sonny. You!' somebody bellowed. 'You! Stop!'

His instinct was to run, like he had from the shop, but the headlights startled him to a standstill. A tall policeman unwound himself from the car and put a hand out towards his shoulder. 'What's your name?'

Be cool. Be calm. You can do it. Speak slow. You can ...

'What's your name, I asked you?'

'Mark Walker,' he said easily.

'Well, Mark Walker, Mr Mark Walker, you can tell us what you're bleedin' well doing cruisin' the streets at 4.30 in the morning.'

Something made Robbie remain cool and calm, though his heart had started thumping again the way it had in the shop. 'Going home,' he said, 'I'm going home.'

'And where might home be?'

It came to him in a flash. Just like magic it came out of the air. The name of her town! And he spoke it with such sureness he knew it sounded right. It did sound like home.

'Lismore. I'm going on the train. From Central.'

'How old are you, sonny?'

'I'm sixteen.'

'And I'm Tom Cruise. Where's your folks?'

'My grandma said I could come home any time. I don't like it in Sydney. I'm going back home.'

'There's a 7.30 out of Central,' the huge man at the wheel of the car spoke now. 'Is that where you're heading? To the station?'

'Yeah, the 7.30,' Robbie said thankfully, 'from Central.'

'Well, just before you go on your way to Lismore— I'm going to have a check of your pockets. There's a place up the way here missing some money. I hope I don't find a big wack of it in your pockets or it won't be Lismore for you.'

'He's clean—only enough there to get him home,' the young officer said to the man at the wheel.

He gave Robbie a shove. 'Get going now. And stay put in Lismore, you hear? With your grandma.'

Robbie ran the rest of the way to the station without raising his head.

The newspapers were already coming in on the huge central platform with all its little shops down one side. He bought himself a hot drink from a kiosk where the woman was noisily raising the shutters. 'Country Trains', he could see the sign from here.

He stood in front of the big departures board, a paper mug of steaming coffee with three sugars in one hand and a Mars Bar in the other, reading the lists of stations. *Newcastle, Taree, Coffs Harbour, Lismore, Kyogle*. He liked the sounds of those country names. NORTHERN EXPRESS PLATFORM 5 at 7.30 am, sure enough.

He sat down to wait on one of the orange plastic benches that snaked their way up and down the station. There were plenty of others still asleep on them. Lots of old men, a few young ones too, and girls, some of them in sleeping bags. But there was no trouble finding a place. It was pretty hard, the seat, but it seemed so warm in here compared to the reservoir. As he lay back, Robbie thought he might have been in heaven.

26
Morning

He wakened to an unfamiliar sight.
A soaring ceiling of corrugated iron,
Held up by a web of metal beams.
Glass windows, set in the iron.
Through the glass he could see sky.
A grey space, interrupted
with odd fluttering movements
now and then.
Birds! Birds flying over the great domed ceiling.
Where was he then?
When he moved he remembered.
(He felt the hard plastic bench beneath him.)
Oh, he was stiff all over!
He moved his bruised shoulder cautiously,
his aching joints,
hurting as they had in that wet, dark tomb he wanted so
much to forget.
The place he'd been buried in for the past two days.

Yes, he was stiff and his body ached.
But his heart was light, light!
He wasn't in that blackness any more.
He was in a place with a domed roof
with birds flying over,
a place that was filled with daylight.

He pushed up his sleeve to check his arm.
Something etched there made him smile,
feel ready for anything.
It was a silvery morning here,
it was going to be a golden day.
He watched the birds again for a moment
against the piece of sky.
Then he sat up, looked around, smiled
and swung his mud-covered joggers to the floor.